Magic Man

Awenmell Characters 1

Lisa King

FELEN PRESS

Felen Press

Magic Man - Awenmell Characters 1

ISBN 978-0-6483026-2-9 (eBook)
ISBN 978-0-6483026-3-6 (Print)

NATIONAL
LIBRARY
OF AUSTRALIA

A catalogue record for this
book is available from the
National Library of Australia

For those with scars

"... Across the fire sits the magic man and his wand. He chuckles and a sadistic grin spreads across his inebriated face. I only have eyes for the straw doll he holds in his hands. He flips it this way and that, pretending to drop it into the fire and catching it, eager for a reaction. It's not that I don't understand the game we are playing. I just don't wish to play...."

- Crown of Fire
Awenmell Series : Book One

1

I t wasn't the ropes themselves that bothered Tabar so much. Their coarse threads had twisted and coiled around each other until they'd made a dense cord almost as thick as his tiny wrists. They looked a bit like the big bracelets he'd seen on fine ladies in Lewtshire; not that the ladies ever found themselves tied in ropes and dragged behind a guard who walked so fast they'd have to take three steps to the guard's one.

Three steps. Tabar had counted them. He knew how to count but he couldn't remember ever learning how. Just like he couldn't remember how he learned to hide in the darkest lanes in Lewtshire and to always keep his head covered. Always.

The guard tugged on the ropes and Tabar stumbled forward, catching his foot on a stone on the dusty roadway. He regained his balance, his heart pumping in fear at almost being dragged along by the guard like a piece of refuse.

Tabar might've escaped the Brennyn guards with the other boys if his hat hadn't fallen off and exposed him.

"Bastard son of the invaders!" they'd called him and smacked his head so hard he wondered if they were trying to slap the white hair from his head. Tabar didn't react to the slur or the punches. He'd endured worse. His hair, and the memories it brought to those who'd survived, needed to be wiped out. He understood that now.

In Lewtshire, he'd heard tales about the vicious invaders; hair like ice with hearts just as cold, evil and corrupt animals who destroyed villages and defiled the women. Tabar didn't know what "defiled" meant, but he knew being one of *them* meant everyone else's past created his future.

He trotted behind the guard and wondered if they fed people before they executed them. Perhaps it wouldn't be so bad to die after all—if you were warm and fed. The guard tugged on the ropes again and Tabar winced. No, it wasn't the ropes that bothered him, it was the way their fibers irritated the half-healed burns along his arms.

The guard's boots crunched into the stones in a solid rhythm, *one, two, one, two,* and when the beat slowed at a rise Tabar lifted his head. Farmhouses appeared closer together, and a short distance away the thatched roofs of a small village popped up behind green hedges like scratchy gray mushrooms.

Tabar stepped closer to the guard, proud of the slack he'd created; it meant the tug he expected didn't affect his wrists at all. Soon a gray stone wall rose along one side of the road. It only came to the guard's waist, but Tabar had trouble seeing over it. The wall was as high as his shoulders and masses of unkempt climbing plants hung over its capstones.

The crunching sound of the guard's boots stopped. Tabar froze after his next step, slowly bringing his feet closer together for balance. Something over the wall had caught the guard's attention, and he stood with his hands on his hips and watched through a small opening that must have once held a gate. Keeping as much distance as he could, Tabar crept around and behind the guard so he might see through the gateway too.

A small thatched house sat amongst overgrown vines. Plots of half-tended produce filled the yard and behind a large spray of a vegetable gone to seed, there was some movement and muttering. The angle of the wall blocked most of Tabar's view but he could tell the muttering belonged to an old lady, and it seemed she was weakly swinging some kind of tool around.

Tabar edged closer to the guard. The short, stout woman wore a kerchief on her head and held an axe in her hand. She tapped at pieces of firewood and muttered to herself, and the guard beside him placed his hand on his chest. The guard was tall and strong; maybe he wasn't so bad after all if he felt pity for an old lady. Tabar bet the guard could chop all the firewood she'd need in one day.

"Right." The guard loosened the heavy ropes around Tabar's wrists and smacked him across the head. "Get in there and help, Dreg!"

Tabar stumbled through the gate as the old lady started and pulled the axe close to her chest.

"Here," the guard called to her as he leaned on the wall, "Use this. I'll head to the tavern and come back for him later."

The old lady stood still, her eyes wide and the axe trembling in her hands. Tabar froze. Why was *she* scared? She was at least double his size and she was the one holding the axe. She didn't take her eyes from Tabar as she spoke. "But he's a . . ."

The guard waved her concern away. "But only a little one. Must be what? Five summers? Can't imagine he'd do much damage." He pulled some cloth from the dirt at the base of the wall and tossed it towards Tabar motioning for him to put it on his head. "Don't shame this house, now."

Tabar waited, his head bowed and covered in rotting cloth, for the old lady to hand him the axe. Her eyes reminded him of someone who once trusted him to do the right thing, someone scared. More than anything, he wanted to prove he *could* do the right thing. Tabar didn't know a lot of things, but he knew how to count, he knew how to cut wood, and he knew what scared looked like. Once the axe was in his hands, the old lady took refuge behind a frame of climbing beans, rubbed at her elbows, and watched him split the wood.

Some pieces split easily, others needed extra taps and bangs to free them from the blunt axe blade. Splinters from the rough timber handle pierced his palms, and sometimes the axe-head seemed so heavy he thought it might fall down his back, so Tabar was sure not to swing it too high. He pretended he didn't notice the old lady move from plant to plant until she was safely inside the door of the cottage.

Soon afterward, she reemerged from the cottage, but with another old lady, this one tall and skinny. "See, Hennie, look," she said and pointed to Tabar. He snuck a glance at the taller lady, who glared at him. The splinters in his hands were softer than her.

Hennie's voice was dry and brittle. "Well, I must say, he's quite strong for a weed . . . I think we should keep him."

Tabar didn't dare look up, even when the smell of the rotting cloth on his head made his nose scrunch up.

"Oh no, we can't do that."

"And why not?"

The short lady whispered into Hennie's ear, as if the truth was too distasteful to speak aloud.

"Oh, is he? What a shame to waste that strength." Tabar peeked at the women as Hennie tapped at her chin. Her neck leaned ahead of her body and her nose pointed like a beak. Tabar wondered if people grew into their names. "Well, we should at least consider it, Flora," she said. "Winter's almost here. Are *you* going to chop all our firewood?"

Flora rubbed at her elbows, and Tabar looked down and chopped the wood harder and faster, ignoring the little cuts on his hands from the axe handle. "It's true," he heard her say. "He'd come in handy, but it's not like he has the strength of a grown man."

"We keep that sow of yours and she has small litters."

"At least she gives us something for the slops. What would *he* do?" Flora looked back at the cottage. "Besides, we don't have room."

Tabar stooped over the wood as he split it. He could be small too. He could be anything they wanted him to be. Blood rushed through his veins and the more he puffed the more he seemed unable to catch his breath.

"Put him with the pig. He might help keep her warm."

"What if my pig doesn't like him? Besides, we can't have one of *them* here. What will people say?"

Hennie strode over to Tabar and rested a curled finger on her chin. She grabbed his shoulder to turn him and Tabar dropped the axe, stretched as tall as he could and tried to slow his breathing. "Would they have to know?" she asked.

Flora crept closer and looked around the garden as if the beans might be spies. "What do you mean?"

Tabar's eyes widened. What on earth *did* she mean? He didn't resist as Hennie wrenched his mouth open and inspected his teeth, then held his eyes open for Flora to see. "Look, he doesn't have their bright-blue eyes."

"Maybe he has the soul of his poor mother."

"Get my shears."

A few moments later, Flora slapped the shears into Hennie's waiting palm. Her other hand already held Tabar by his hair. Tabar pushed down his last remaining spark of panicked energy. The panic had never helped him before, only teased him with escape when none was possible. He thought he'd hang; how strange to be disappointed that an old lady and a blade would be his end. Warm liquid ran down Tabar's leg and pooled in his shoe. Would they even notice? They seemed more interested in the clumps of his hair that lay on the ground anyway.

Hennie reached into the soil and scrubbed a handful into his shortened hair. "See? Keep him dirty. No one will know."

Flora turned him by his shoulders, bent towards him, and for the first time addressed him directly. "You wouldn't hurt my sow, would you?"

Tabor was as terrified of pigs as he was of fire. He shook his head.

Hennie pulled a coin from a fold in her apron and pushed it into Flora's hand. "Go to the tavern. Tell the guard the dreg ran away."

Hennie's shears slashed at Tabar's hair as he watched Flora waddle along the road toward the village. When she disappeared, he focused on the plants that hung over the gray wall; they were spindly, but still alive. He tried his hardest not to jump when Hennie cut his scalp or to scratch at the blood as it tickled its way down his neck.

Tabar squeezed his lips together and tried not to smile. He thought for a moment that he might even be dreaming.

Tabar had a home.

L ater that day, as the whip stung his back again, tears dripped from the end of Tabar's nose. The flagstones around the hearth in the widows' cottage were laid unevenly, and the edges dug into his skin as he knelt on them. He couldn't tell whether the chill that ached them came from the stones themselves or from the cold breeze seeping into the cottage. He jumped as Hennie brought the switch down again.

"What a waste of time," she moaned to Flora. "If he can't even start a fire, what good is he?"

Flora looked up from her stitching frame and pulled a blanket closer to her shoulders. "And I'd just got used to this grand idea. You're always so clever, Hennie; it's not your fault if it won't work."

The flint trembled in Tabar's hand. His knees felt icy, but perspiration dotted his brow, and he felt sure he had lost his mind. How could it be that each scrape of the flint took him out of the widows' cottage and transported him back to Lewtshire? Was it some kind of evil magic?

He struck the flint again, just as Hennie's switch bit into his shoulder. The sparks almost took to the char cloth, but just like every other time, Tabar panicked and snuffed it out. The next strike took and caught the moss alongside the char cloth alight in the tiniest flame. Tabar screamed at its presence and the sting of Hennie's wrath kept time with the scrape of the flint.

Each spark drew him closer to the memories of the burns that ran up and down his arms. Punishment. He wasn't even sure what for. The older boys who ran in the lanes of Lewtshire said he didn't follow their instructions, or bring them what they wanted, even when he'd been extra careful. Sometimes there was no reason. Maybe they just liked to hear him scream.

Tabar wailed with every spark that flew from the flint to the char cloth and moss and every beat of Hennie's switch. The burns along his arms stung in panic of what was sure to come. The tiny flames, extinguished by his tears or blown away by his screams, never made it to the tinder, let alone the kindling. Hennie grabbed his shoulders and Tabar, convinced he was being held down in Lewtshire, broke from her grasp, stood and shrieked. He panted, as desperately as he might if he'd just run for his life, and, wide eyed, placed himself back in the widows' home. He *wasn't* in Lewtshire, no matter what his body told him.

"I don't know what you're screeching about." Hennie shook her head at him. "I stopped hitting you a while ago." She reached for him again. "You're useless. You'll have to go."

No! Tabar knew he could prove himself. He could be anything they needed him to be. Anything that would keep him from the guards or from Lewtshire. He dropped to the hearth and struck at the flint over and over again, but nothing took, not even the tiniest of flames. The burns on his arms flared with irritation at each strike and he could see the lanes of Lewtshire in his mind, but he kept his eye on the hearth, the sparks, and the flint in his hand.

Hennie pulled him to his feet and shook the flint from his hand. It rattled onto the floor as she dragged him by the wrist toward the door.

"Look, Hennie!" Hennie stopped and turned, still holding Tabar. Flora pointed to the hearth and the wisp of smoke that hovered between being taken up or being extinguished in the moss. A small flame popped its head through the dry fibers.

Flame! In an instant, what had always meant terror transformed into his relief. Tabar tore himself from Hennie's grasp and coaxed the flame from moss to tinder to kindling to fire. He concentrated hard and gave it enough food to grow and space to breathe, and it rewarded him with a sting of heat to his face.

Cold air whipped along the floor of the cottage and turned Tabar's red cheeks from the fire. Hennie stood at the door. "You've done your job. Off to your lodgings."

Flora chuckled. "Lodgings. What a fine sense of humor you have." She waved her stitching at Tabar as he passed. "Here," she said, and handed him a lump of dark bread as big as his hand. "Wait. Don't you hurt my pig, mind. Make sure she's happy."

Tabar shook his head, then nodded, then shook it again. He was glad they didn't ask him a question; his throat was so dry he was sure he couldn't speak.

How was he supposed to keep a pig happy?

Tabar considered sleeping outside. A small amount of light shone from the window of the house, and the blue-gray of dusk hung over the disused fields, only darkening for the rain-clouds in the distance. A gust of cold air stung the back of his neck and the idea shivered its way out of him.

"Lazy wind," he mumbled, and folded his arms around himself. One of the boys in Lewtshire had told him that some winds are too lazy to go around you, so they go right through you. He imagined him huddled somewhere in a back alley and wondered if the winds were lazy in Lewtshire that night too.

The sty lay half a field away from the widow's cottage, its low wall of gray stones not unlike the wall at the front of the house yard, and the remainder of its height made up of a collection of odd-sized boards that reached to the sloping roof. Tabar thought of Lewtshire, and the sty didn't look so bad after all.

The wind rattled the loose boards that made up the full-sized gate. Tabar slid his fingers along the gaps and thought of ways he might stop the wind coming through. On the other side of the gate, the pig lay as a mass on the far side of the stall. She lifted her head and grunted, a deep, guttural sound that froze Tabar to the spot. The smell of old vegetables reached his nostrils, and he spied leftover husks and grain among the straw on the floor. He let out the breath he didn't even know he held. She'd already eaten.

Tabar leaned on the gate and felt the lump of bread in his pocket. For a moment he thought about eating it outside, but the occasional *blip-blip* of the rain became steady and he'd have no way to dry himself. There was no worse combination; cold *and* wet. He pushed the gate further and slid himself into the sty, his mouth too dry to think of bread, and his heart beating in his ears.

The pig lifted her head, and he stood still and hoped he might magically blend into the walls. He waited for her to move, and tried not to breathe, one hand on the gate, ready to escape. She shuffled in her hay and made noises too loud for such a small amount of effort, eventually laying her head down when she seemed convinced Tabar was no threat.

Tabar scanned the barn in the looming darkness. Some of the straw on the floor was wet and smelly, but the sight of some patches that seemed fresh and inviting made his legs feel heavy and tired. Soft straw was the closest he'd ever come to a warm embrace. For each side step he took toward it, the pig shuffled and rumbled, and as he slid his back down the lumpy stone wall, he kept his eyes on her form as she snuffled and repositioned her head.

She seemed scarier at eye level, even on the other side of the sty. Tabar was sure she must be three times his size, and he'd have no chance if she chose to eat him. The only other pigs he'd seen were in crates in Lewtshire, and they screamed and grunted and made so much noise he'd always covered his ears and run away. Sometimes he dreamed of two-headed pigs that screeched and swooped on him with lots of teeth. This pig only had one head, and he didn't want to know anything about her teeth.

He waited for her to settle until she was still and motionless. The wind hissed through small cracks in the wall and stung his back, so he quietly grabbed a handful of straw and stuffed it behind him. The pig lifted her head and grunted in short stabs into the air. Tabar's every muscle tensed. Could he make it to the gate before her? She kept grunting, louder than before. The widows would think he'd upset her. "Shh!" he said, and she stopped, but then a discontented grumble rolled through her whole body. *Oh no!*

She rose, her huge flank lifting into the air, and once she was on four feet, shook her whole body. She was as big as a water barrel—with legs and teeth—and headed straight to Tabar, grunting and rumbling. Tabar folded his head to his knees and hugged them as close as he could to his body. *She's already eaten. She's already eaten.*

Her leathery snout sniffed and bounced over his body. It would have tickled him if Tabar wasn't tensed and ready for her bite. Her breath was warm on his scalp and he raised his shoulders as she snuffled along the back of his neck, looking for the best place to sink her teeth. She nuzzled her way over his body as if searching for something... *The bread!*

Tabar relaxed his knee, giving her access to the bread in his pocket, and she tugged and pulled at it until it was free. She chomped and chewed in satisfaction, and Tabar's stomach rumbled at the smell of the bread as it disappeared forever. He peeked out through his arms as she nodded in enjoyment. She sniffed him over again, much to Tabar's alarm; how could he explain there was no more bread?

Her next series of grunts rolled into a long sighing sound, and she flopped next to him in the hay. Tabar stayed very still as she made herself comfortable. Her last sigh was so contented and long, Tabar felt the heat of her breath on his leg. Once she was breathing steadily, he watched her closely. Twilight had removed all the color from the day, but he could still make out his pale fist. He looked at her ears. He could put his whole fist down there. Nothing about her was soft; her eyelashes looked like the bristles from a stiff broom, and her feet were like clubs. Perhaps it was only because he couldn't move, but Tabar sat with the pig, and with his fear, until they were no longer enemies.

In the following moons, Tabar listened as the widows complained about the unseasonal weather, the rains and storms that lashed the land, and shook their heads when they learned that a valley had flooded. Tabar tried to imagine how much water that would take. He had his own troubles trying to find high and dry spots in the sty. When it rained for days, the sty flooded and the barn stank. It wasn't only the pig that smelled—the mold that grew on the wood and walls seemed to thicken the air so much he could feel it in his body and taste it in the air. He knew this was probably nowhere near as bad as a whole valley full of water.

In between the bouts of rain, Tabar took the pig out of the sty and let her forage around in the forest for whatever pigs found interesting. He collected mosses, wood, and kindling, dried them as best he could, and practiced lighting fires. Soon he knew which fuels took quickly and which ones burned hottest and longest, and he could light a fire under almost any conditions. He didn't *like* fire, he wasn't sure that he ever would, but he did like what it had brought to him.

Although the widows didn't say it, Tabar liked to imagine they were pleased with him. They always seemed satisfied when the fire burst into life on particularly miserable days, when he could take damp kindling and make fire out of nothing. On those days, after he lit the fire he tried to stay still and dared not make a sound, but they always remembered he was there in front of their fire and sent him back to the pig.

2

After a couple of summers, Tabar considered himself half grown. He could light any fire with ease, collect and chop firewood, tend to Flora's pig, and work the widows' vegetable beds. He was always sure to wear his oversized cap; it didn't take too many of Hennie's switches for him to fear a cool breeze on his head. Sometimes he would lean into the widows' hands while they checked the length of his hair and they would slap him for his familiarity. He learned instead to appreciate the few moments when they accidentally touched his skin.

In that short amount of time, while Tabar was busy growing, the widows grew older and slower. One morning, they called him into the cottage.

"Stand there." Hennie ordered, pointing to the middle of the room. Tabar stood still as both women studied him, Hennie rubbing her chin and Flora tipping her head from one side to the other.

Flora's head bounced in a series of quick nods. "I think it will work." She reached beside her stitching chair and pulled out a pair of pants and a shirt she'd altered. "These were my husband's," she said. Tabar wasn't sure what he was supposed to say or do. "Well?" Flora shook the clothes at him. "Take your clothes off."

The clothes were old but felt new against his skin. He sniffed the shirt on his arm, and it smelt a little like ale, but at least it didn't smell like the pig. The widows were still surveying him.

Flora pulled his cap down so it covered most of his face. "That'll have to do."

"Wait." Hennie bent to the hearth and took some ashes in her fingertips. She smeared them over Tabar's eyebrows as he blinked against the dust falling into his eyes. "Much better." The widows stood back to admire their work and Hennie clasped her skinny hands together. "Today you will walk with us to the village and we will show you where, and how, to collect anything we might need."

The village? Tabar felt as though the walls of their cottage had unfolded and left him alone with a cool breeze blowing across his head. What if he was found? His heart beat so hard he could feel its rhythm in his hands. He held them close to his chest, scared they might burst.

"Wait outside." Hennie said and pointed to the door.

Tabar folded his chin over his hands and tried to squeeze the pulsing away from them as he left the room.

Tabar knew the village was only a short walk away. He'd seen the roofs of its houses when he'd been in the back field with the pig. He followed the widows through the gate of the gray wall and rubbed at his wrists as he stepped onto the road. It was just as rocky as he remembered, but as they got closer to the village, it smoothed to smaller stones, and then to tempered earth as they entered the gates.

Houses lined the main road, made of either stone or timber, and they all shared the same gray roofs he could see from the field. The road was wide enough for two carts to pass if they were slow and careful, yet when Tabar peeked out from under his cap, people going about their business filled most of its space. The villagers waved or nodded at the widows, and he was grateful that most seemed to ignore his presence and didn't notice he trembled with each step. They stopped outside a butchery. A large barrel of salt stood inside the door and flies dotted the old blood splashes on the stone threshold.

"Now pay attention," Hennie said as they entered.

She placed her order with the butcher and without looking in Tabar's direction she stretched her arm toward him and told the butcher, "On occasion, this..." She stumbled on what to call him.

Flora interjected with, "He helps us. Yes, he's our helper."

"As I was saying, our *helper* may occasionally run errands. You may provide him with what we need."

The butcher looked down at Tabar. The boy peeked out from under his cap and hoped the butcher couldn't see his ash-covered eyebrows. "A helper, you say?" he said to Tabar. "An honorable position."

Hennie snorted and shoved Tabar toward the door then pushed past him, leaving him no choice but to follow her march out the door, with Flora following close behind. "The butcher thinks the boy is some kind of orphan that is being honorable by helping us," she hissed at Flora.

Flora trotted behind her sister. "Isn't that a good thing?"

"But they'll all start gossiping."

"At least they'll be gossiping about that, and not what he *really* is."

Hennie stopped right in the middle of the road and Flora marched straight into her. By the time Flora had apologized, Hennie had decided it was best the villagers believed Tabar was an orphan. The widows wouldn't lie, but they wouldn't correct the village gossip either. At each store they selected, they introduced Tabar as their helper, and they knew within a day or two they wouldn't have to explain his presence again.

Tabar wasn't sure if it was the delightful warmth or the smell of bread that made the bakery the gathering place of the village. He'd followed the widows past the busy tavern, which seemed filled with farmers; not the type of people here at the bakery, which was full of travelers and law makers and people that talked a lot.

He squeezed his way through the crowd, hoping to not lose sight of the widows who parted the throng with ease. Occasionally an elbow tapped at his hat, but he made sure to hold it down. People argued in corners about laws and waved sticks of bread at each other, and he heard half snippets of conversations about trade and medicines. These people used so many words he'd never heard before. If the widows sent him here, he'd learn much more than to count.

Tabar followed the widows closely, and the crowd closed in behind them as they passed. They halted at a bench tended by a burly man with a cloth on his head, knotted in each corner to keep it in place over tight dark curls. Behind him, a large clay oven baked bread, and toward the back of the bakery, a smaller open fire burned under a large pot hanging on a tripod.

"Ah, widows. We hope you are well today," he said above the noise.

Someone surged behind them, and the jostle moved like a wave among everyone, pushing Tabar's chest into the counter. "We are well," Hennie began and almost touched Tabar as she introduced him to the baker. Tabar imagined all the baker saw was the top of his cap.

A young girl's voice, angry and sharp, rose from behind the baker and his eyes widened. Red-faced, the baker stomped toward the voice and lifted his arms. "Mahkishla!" he yelled, "Bite your tongue!" Tabar ducked and waited for the sound of blows but was relieved the baker's actions were only in exasperation.

Tabar didn't know what she'd said to upset him but voices in the crowd had their own interpretations.

"Again?" they moaned. Some huffed, and the widows lowered and shook their heads.

Another voice called, "You'd do best to keep her under control. Look how she upsets your customers," and others murmured their agreement.

The baker turned back to the widows, wiped his brow with a cloth, and smiled almost apologetically. Behind him, Tabar couldn't quite make out what the girl said as she waved her arms around. Although she looked around the same age as him, it seemed she had a lot more to say than he ever did and was clearly upset. She took a long, deep breath and stood still.

The girl named Mahkishla now fell quiet, but one eyebrow remained raised and she clenched her jaw. She looked like she was made out of stone, but to Tabar, the hardness of her stance only made her black wavy hair look softer as it fell past her shoulders.

The man beside Tabar yelled, "If she won't bite her tongue, perhaps you should cut it out!" The crowd pressed again, and the thought they might actually do it terrified Tabar. But Mahkishla didn't run; if anything, she seemed to stand firmer right where she was next to the fire. She wasn't scared of it at all.

"She'll bring you nothing but sorrow with that mouth of hers," another voice called.

Did that tripod leg just wobble? Yes, it did. Tabar's eyes followed one of the thin metal legs to where it balanced on a pile of loose boards. The damaged leg was shorter than the others and as the fire grew hotter, the leg slid on the boards. Tabar's mouth opened as the tripod leaned to its side and then dropped the pot and its contents onto the fire below. A cloud of steam rose in its place. Mahkishla didn't even look at the fire—she stood beside it as if she'd commanded it all to happen herself.

"Mahkishla!" the baker yelled. "The fire!" But she just stood there.

"Insolence!" a customer cried and pushed himself toward the bench, a raised horse whip in his hand. Mahkishla didn't move, she didn't even duck or flinch. The baker reached up to stop the blow, and the widows pushed Tabar forward.

"He'll re-start your fire. He's like magic. He can set anything on fire," Flora said.

"A magic man?" someone in the crowd guffawed.

Hennie turned to face the smirking crowd, and her stare transformed their smiles to serious nods. "Watch," she said.

Tabar made his way around the bench, dipped his head as he passed the baker and fell to his knees next to the wet wood. He may have been out of the crush but he still couldn't breathe with all eyes in the bakery fixed on him. Would his hands work with the beat of his heart back inside them? He reached for the flint, and even with his back to the crowd, he tensed against their eyes that transformed into pointed fingers.

He pulled his cap down and surveyed the damage. A piece of broken metal nearby made a great scraper to remove the thin outer layers that had soaked in the spill and expose the dry wood underneath. There wasn't much liquid to deal with, and he'd worked with wood more sodden than this before. He kept scraping, knowing that once the fire was alight it would burn slowly for a while, but would soon dry the remaining pieces as if the spill had never occurred.

Tabar snorted. He wasn't magic. He was just doing what needed to be done. It might seem that way to others, he supposed. If knowing what to do made you magic, then this village needed more help than he thought. He used some dry shavings to coax the new fire to life.

The baker bowed. "Thank you, widows," he said, and the hum of conversation returned to the bakery. Tabar exhaled as the pointing fingers disappeared from his back. He breathed the warm air deeply and pretended to tend the fire, perspiration trickling down his temple. Not having a rag handy, he wiped it away with the back of his hand and tensed at the sight of the black smear of charcoal that he had unwittingly wiped from his eyebrows.

He bowed his head before the fire. If he turned, they would discover him and the widows would think he had purposely shamed them. Tabar closed his eyes to think but could only hear the conversations behind him. The chatter sounded dull, like people were murmuring or humming, and even if someone shouted it was soft, like something cloth-wrapped. His hands thumped with the beat of his heart as they rested on his thighs.

He felt a tap on his leg and frowned. He opened his eyes to find Mahkishla had sidled next to him; their legs were almost touching as they knelt at the fire. He offered her a sideways glance, his heart beating so hard it hurt everywhere now, not just his hands. If she saw his eyebrows, she would tell with that big mouth of hers, right here in front of everyone. She nudged his leg again with her fist and slowly opened her hand. Inside were cooled ashes from the fire.

"Come along now!" the widows called for him, and he pinched the ashes from the girl's hand and rubbed them on his brow.

They stood, and he nodded in thanks and Mahkishla smiled and stood tall. "I told him that tripod would fall," she said. Then she raised her voice for all to hear, "But no one ever listens to me!"

"Mahkishla!" the baker boomed. "Bite your tongue!"

Tabar ducked under the baker's words and hurried to the widows but there was a new warmth inside him, as if some part of the fire had jumped from the kindling to inside his body.

3

The only time Tabar was freed from the watchful eyes of the widows was when they told him to wash the pig. He thought it strange they seemed to only remember the pig needed washing when he stood close to them inside their house— and thought it strange that people washed their pigs at all. But still, the order to *go wash the pig*' meant a break from his work and a swim in the small stream that ran a few fields beside the widow's property.

A tall dead tree marked his favorite place to swim. It stood next to a bend in the stream that had created a pool of slow-moving water that came up to his waist. After his swim, Tabar dressed and lay on the low pebbled bank beside a small grove of trees. The pig slid in the grass along the bank and shoveled the rich dark dirt with her nose. He had come to understand her expressive eyes, but she was always prickly on the outside and unpleasant to touch, and he laughed out loud when he realized how much pigs were like people.

A stick cracked in the grove beside him and Tabar slapped his cap to his head.

He sat still and strained to hear. He hoped it was a wild animal; it would be safer for him if it was. The pig rooted around among some reeds and hadn't seemed to notice anything, yet Tabar still sensed something, or someone, was there. He feigned interest in the pebbles at his side and glanced into the grove long enough to see dark hair disappear behind a trunk. He felt sure he heard a gasp, and he was almost as sure that this visitor was the baker's daughter. *Visitor?* It was probably he and the pig that had disturbed her. He pretended he didn't hear the crack, the gasp, or see her hair.

"Does she bite?" Mahkishla stepped out from behind a tree but held onto it for good measure, her eyes fixed on the pig that still rooted around among the reeds.

"Sometimes. If she's tired or gets boisterous."

"Does it hurt?"

"Depends on where she bites, I suppose."

The stream rippled quietly by while Tabar tried to figure out if he should say anything else, and Mahkishla tried to find the right words. The pig broke the silence as she grunted and snorted excitedly about something she'd discovered in the reeds, and Mahkishla found her voice.

"My father says I'm not to talk to you."

Tabar nodded, watching the stream. He turned his attention to the pig, expecting to hear Mahkishla's footsteps disappearing back through the grove.

Her feet crunched into the stones on the bank and stopped next to him. "But I'm no good at doing what I'm told."

"I'd noticed that," he said and smiled, his eyes still on the stream.

"He says it's because of the pigs but I'm not stupid; I know it's more than that."

"You do?"

"It's because you're one of *them*."

One of them. Tabar knew better than to think anyone would see beyond who he was. His label. He couldn't argue with her statement. Even if he was just *part* of one of them, he was still a reminder. He wondered if he was found. "If he knows what I am, why doesn't he send me away—or worse?"

She shrugged and sat next to him. "Maybe it's because you help the widows and don't cause him any trouble."

"Unlike you."

She smiled smugly at him. Tabar imagined her on the streets and back lanes of Lewtshire running for her life. He didn't like to judge people, but she'd be no good at hiding. Her and that mouth of hers. It was a good thing she wasn't born with white hair.

Mahkishla chose a pebble and tossed it into the water. "I think you're the only person in this village that hasn't rolled their eyes at me or said, 'Oh, your poor father!'"

"Don't you think you should avoid trouble and not upset everyone?"

"I thought you were different than them."

"I'm pretty sure I am." Tabar thought about the whippings and the burns and the fact that he slept with a pig. "Yes, I'm sure I am."

"Well, it seems to me you're just like everyone else. 'Hush, Mahkishla! Bite your tongue, Mahkishla!'"

He liked her impersonation. "They do say that a lot, don't they?"

She nodded then leaned closer to him and whispered her secret. "I can't help it. The ideas and thoughts come out of my mouth sometimes before my mind knows it. Sometimes I bite on my tongue so hard, I taste blood in my mouth."

Tabar was scared for her. She was small, made to work in a large bakery filled with angry adults, and yet there was something strong about her, like she was bigger than she appeared. Tabar pulled his sleeves up and scratched at his head, but he still couldn't figure it out.

Mahkishla lay her arm alongside his and pointed to the burns on her arms. "I got mine from the bakery fire. It's because I'm not careful enough. How did you get yours?"

Tabar stretched his arm next to hers. Their skin touched from shoulder to wrist and Lewtshire faded from his mind, as if washed away as easily as the dirt from his body in the stream. Everything seemed new and fresh. "I guess I wasn't careful enough either."

Mahkishla jumped to her feet and put her hands on her hips. "Here's what you will do. When you come here to swim, you'll hang your shirt on the low bough of that dead tree. I'll see it from the bakery and I can come talk to you without the adults knowing."

Tabar couldn't imagine what they'd have to talk about. He thought her plan was more about getting all those words and ideas out of her insides without being told to shut up. But he didn't mind. Her plan meant he'd have someone to talk to, and he could do most of the listening.

M any summers had passed, but this one was long, and the pond almost dry. The old pig struggled to the water's edge while one of her daughters was belly deep in the mud and green water. The widows had ignored Tabar's suggestion they keep one of her litter— until they had the brilliant idea themselves to do just that.

Tabar left his shirt draped on the tree; a different branch now that the old bough had broken in a storm many summers ago. Tending more of the property for the aging widows had broadened Tabar's back, and although he kept his hat close for his frequent trips to the village, his hair had darkened enough to not cause a stranger concern at first sight. Now that he had grown, he used a blade to keep his hair short and his face clean-shaven.

Mahkishla snuck up behind him as he sat on the bank. He pretended not to hear her feet on the dry stones and acted startled when she put her hands on his shoulders and planted a kiss on his cheek.

He held her hand and pulled her beside him. "How goes the village today, Kish?"

"Busy. I won't be able to stay for long, and look, I got another burn today." She pulled bread from a sack, then showed him the angry blisters. "Almost as good as yours, Magic Man." Kish hadn't grown out of being loudmouthed and opinionated, but she'd never asked Tabar anything else about his burns, as if she knew something about deep burns that other people didn't. That you remember every single one of them, and how they came to be.

Tabar winced at the sight of the welts on her arm. "Oh, Kish." He couldn't remember when he'd started calling her Kish, and she hadn't complained once. He wondered if she knew 'ma kish' meant "my pulse," but he was too afraid to ask.

Kish divided the bread and hurriedly finished chewing the piece she'd put in her mouth. "I heard about a new village today, and I've decided I'm going to live there... one day."

Tabar pulled the crust from his mouth. "You are?"

"I am." She picked at the soft bread in the center of the loaf. "Tunstream. They're building it in that valley where the old village was washed away in the floods. Word among the travelers and traders is that it's a stupid idea, but it intrigues me. Can you imagine? They're rebuilding something new, on something that was old and washed away. Like a second chance or something."

"How are you going to manage that? Don't you have to stay here and be the baker's daughter and marry a baker?" Tabar frowned against the stinging thought of Kish with someone else. Besides, she had everything she could want. A home where she was warm and fed, and a family, people that cared. Why would she leave?

"I want to do more than bake bread and listen to the old ways. I want to go and make new ways myself."

Tabar nodded. Of course, she did. He reached over and collected a flake of crust that had fallen into the waves of her hair and smiled to himself. He should know by now that his Kish didn't do anything she didn't want to, particularly if someone told her she *had* to. That was just asking for trouble. "Tell me about this village."

"I don't know that much about it, really."

"How do you imagine it to be then?"

"Hmm, friendly. Just. A place where I'm heard."

With the bread finished, Tabar lay back on the pebbles. The sun had warmed them, and they massaged his back as he moved. It seemed to him that Kish wanted everything that her village wasn't. "Did you count how many times they told you to bite your tongue today?"

She sighed and looked at the sky. "I gave up counting."

"You gave up? Impossible."

"I'm starting to think some things are worth giving up on. Like, there are some things worth the fight, and others not so much." Tabar watched her face as the thought ran its course through her mind. She frowned, teared up, then smiled and sighed again. "They just don't understand new ideas." She picked a large pebble and tossed it into the pond, the splash sending a rotten waft on the air. "They're like this stinking, stagnant pond. Ugh! I can't believe the pigs still go in there."

Tabar closed his eyes against the sun. "Well, I think your ideas are the most wondrous things I've ever heard."

"You do? Which ones?"

"All of them. They're all about making the villagers think for themselves, aren't they?"

"You'd think they'd handed over their brains along with their sheaves and quotas." Kish picked up another pebble but decided against throwing it into the pond. "Something about a new thought—thinking anything other than what the Hall tells them to think—terrifies them. How can they hear anything I say when their fear is so busy telling me to shut up?" Kish pounded the pebble into the ground at her feet. "Why does the Hall place more value on some people than others? – *Bite your tongue, Mahkishla!* Why do we pretend that it's not actually fear that makes us follow the Hall's traditions? *Shut your mouth, Mahkishla!*" I just don't know how to get them to listen."

"I know you'll find a way." Tabar stood, helped her to her feet, and collected her sack from the pebbles. "And when you find it, I think your ideas could change the world."

Kish stared at Tabar and he wondered for a moment if she hadn't understood what he said. She grabbed his face and kissed his lips. "I love you, Tabar!"

Tabar ducked and checked if they were alone. "Don't say that out loud."

Kish walked back toward the village and wagged her finger. "Don't you start telling me what I can and cannot do, and what I can and can't say."

He watched her weave her way through the grove of trees.

She was going to change the world.

Of course she was. There could be no other way.

"**I**t's happened again!" Hennie called out to Tabar as he worked in the field.

He waved to her and soon after he gathered his favorite flints from inside the widow's home.

"I just don't understand." Flora shook her head. "Since the baker got ill, that silly girl just can't keep the fire lit."

As Tabar approached the bakery he heard raised voices, and a smile crept across his lips. *Again, Kish?* He increased his pace and turned into the lane just as Kish shouted at a trader climbing into his cart. She waved a fire poker above her head.

"I'll accept correction. My father taught me there's always something new to learn!" she shouted, "but I'll never accept your criticism or your ridicule. No matter how you choose to package them, they came from you, and they'll always belong to you!" She raised the poker higher, and if Tabar had not known better, he would have turned his heels at the sight of her.

"Your poor father," the trader said and shook his head. "No wonder he's ill."

Tabar ran the last few strides and clasped his hand around Kish's so she couldn't release the poker. Eventually she calmed enough to realize it was Tabar that held her and relented, handed him the poker, and let him lead her back into the bakery.

"I worry about you," Tabar said as he closed the door. "Some of those Muscone traders would be far less kind than that man was."

Kish turned on him, her anger flashed, and she stabbed the air with her finger. "Are you telling me to be quiet?"

Tabar knew better than most how much it meant for Kish to be heard. "Never! But..."

"But what?"

"Could there be another way? One that doesn't get people so upset?" Kish dragged a lump of dough across the bench and pushed her fist deep into it. He could tell she was biting her tongue. "See that? What you're doing there?"

Kish looked around. She wasn't doing anything but working the dough.

"Punching down. Isn't that what you call it? That's what I imagine people think you're doing to them."

Kish laughed. "It looks harsh, but it's quite gentle, really. It creates a finer grain."

"Maybe you should stop punching down."

Kish worked the dough and shook her head. "It's necessary. It's the only way to create a finer loaf."

Tabar nodded. There was no easy way. No short cuts. Creating finer loaves of the people around her was what she driven to do.

Tabar lit the fire, fed and stoked it, not that Kish needed any help with that, and left her to her kneading. When she'd pushed all her complaints into the dough, she turned her head back to him and the fire.

"Do you think what he said was true?" she asked.

"I was too far away. I didn't hear."

"He complained long and hard about *everything* here. That I shouldn't move things around, that everything should stay the same. I thought he was probably *trying* to make me upset. So I stayed calm. He complained that my father hadn't given me away yet, that he would take me if no one else would."

Tabar smiled because he knew what was coming.

"I tried to stay polite, I really did. But then he said there was so much wrong with me that anyone who enjoyed my company must have something awfully wrong with them... You like me, don't you, Tabar?"

"You know I do."

"But that's what I don't understand. There's nothing wrong with you."

"There's nothing wrong with you either."

Tabar stood beside the fire and watched her punch down another loaf, kneading and refining her thoughts. He'd never again ask her to be something she was not.

4

The widows died one after the other. Of course, Hennie went in her sleep first, to show Flora how to die correctly, and Flora followed a few weeks later. Tabar tidied their home for the last time. He moved the wood basket closer to the fire, where he felt it should have been all along, and took Hennie's switch down from the wall and flung it far into the field.

He ate their bread by candlelight until he was sure his stomach would burst and made a bed for himself out of their blankets on the cottage floor. He tried to imagine what it must have been like to sleep inside every night. It was almost a shame it was a warm summer's evening; he would have enjoyed it more if the night had been bitter.

Early the next morning Tabar opened to door to Kish's pale face. He shrugged and tried to swallow the lump in his throat. "Time to move on, I expect."

Kish pushed past him into the cottage. "There's no chance of you staying?" She didn't wait for his response. "Stay."

Tabar shook his head and followed her inside. "They know what I am here, Kish. To them I'll always be that bastard created in hate and raised in a pig pen by a couple of old widows."

"That's only because they decided *what* you are, not *who* you are—I'll go with you!"

"No, you won't!" Tabar pushed the blankets along the floor with his feet. "All I can provide is ridicule."

"But so many summers have passed since the invasion." Kish picked up Flora's stitching and considered it before dropping it on the chair. "You'd think the hatred would die with the old ones... Tunstream! We'll go to Tunstream. Remember?"

Her eyes were hopeful but Tabar needed her to see sense. "When was the last time you heard anyone speak of it? It might not even exist."

"Just because the traders say there's no profit going into the valley doesn't mean it's not there. We'll go and make a difference, help them build something new... change the world."

"*You* can do that. I won't be changing anything."

He knew that flick in her eye. Kish clenched her fists and lost any battle she was waging against keeping her voice down. "So this is all right for you? The way you're treated? Hiding like you're somehow less of a person because of the color of your hair or the circumstances of your birth? Your value as a person in this village has gone up and down like a commodity. For years, your hair hasn't mattered in the least when fences needed repairing, but you're conveniently *one of them* when it serves their needs best. Doesn't it bother you that the Hall shouts or beats down any new or better way because they fear losing their power?" Tabar was used to her outbursts, yet still closed an eye shut as she continued. "We are on the verge of destroying each other just because they tell us to, and if something doesn't directly affect these villagers, it doesn't matter. But it does. It sits like a cloud over all of us. Can you feel it? I can. Don't you care about your future?"

"Right now, my future consists of *this* day... maybe tomorrow if I'm feeling luxurious."

"You need to care that the Hall is destroying our future!"

"I don't need to care about anything; it's not my problem."

"Your *future* is not your problem?"

"Even if I wanted to, what could I do? Look at me, Kish!" Tabar raised his voice along with his arms. "If I spoke, if I did *anything,* what would they say? What do you expect their reaction to be? I'm so low I'm not even considered lowborn! This would have to be the most idiotic idea you've ever come up with!"

Tears stung at Kish's eyes, and her voice wavered but she continued. "One person *can* make a difference, Tabar! How do you know what one act might set in motion? What if everyone felt like you, that their voice didn't matter? Their insights, their ideas? Nothing would ever change, nothing would ever get done. One decision *can* change your life; maybe even change the village—change the entire world." Kish quietened and stared at Tabar as if she'd finally understood something. "I have to believe that one person can make a difference, Tabar. I have to believe I have a purpose."

A purpose. He knew Kish had a purpose. He could tell just watching the passion build within her, and he would not get in its way. Maybe there were old ladies and pigs in Tunstream who needed help too. He tried to speak, but she'd already started again, or perhaps she hadn't even stopped.

"Well, I'm going," she announced and walked to the doorway. "All this time when I was talking to you, I was really talking to myself! I'm going to Tunstream whether you come or not." She stopped just outside the door, turned and leaned back into the cottage. "I can talk all I want, but I can't be *proud* of thoughts and ideas. My purpose is in my actions. There's no pride in ideas, Tabar, only in their execution."

And she stormed off through the widows' garden and left him standing there.

I t took Tabar most of the day to finalize the widows' accounts with the traders and lodge their property intentions with the village chamber. Most nodded a careful farewell at the end of their business, which was as close to a well-wishing as he might expect, yet there were others where he only breathed freely once out of their presence.

He planned his final stop for the bedside of the old baker. The baker's mind had taken leave several summers ago, as jumbled as the different colors at leaf-fall, but it was only in recent times that his body had forced him into his sickbed. Hordle, his apprentice, greeted Tabar at the door with a firm handshake.

"Is he sleeping?" Tabar asked.

"On and off. Some moments he is full of lightning, others I listen for his next breath."

"I might bid him farewell."

"I wouldn't bother. He hasn't made a skerrick of sense or recognized anyone in moons."

"You've been very patient, Hordle. Has Kish thanked you?"

Hordle's eyes darted to Tabar's but didn't hold his look. "She did."

Tabar patted Hordle's shoulder and smiled as he moved past him. Employing Hordle was one of the wisest decisions the baker ever made. Hordle's transfer from the guild was a very public attempt at matchmaking, and even the villagers remarked how well Kish and Hordle worked together. To the baker's dismay, nothing eventuated, other than Kish's delight at discovering the new apprentice was far more interested in the village tailor than he would ever be in her. Hordle now cared for the old baker in his last days, bringing him familiar baked goods and attending to his needs. Tabar admired the man's patience; the bakery would soon be his. Even more, he admired his discretion—it was obvious he knew Kish had already departed, yet he didn't betray her confidence even to him.

In the darkened room, Tabar sat beside the pallet bed and shook the old man's hand. "Thank you, baker, for your kindness. I am on my way now."

The baker's brow furrowed, and he squinted hard at Tabar. "Here!" he said and rummaged among his blankets, eventually holding a small bun aloft. "Fresh today... but we're all out of currants. You weren't quick enough for the currants! I baked these myself." He held the bun out to Tabar and continued to search his bedclothes.

"I'm sure you did. I should go now." Tabar rose and waited for some kind of recognition before taking his leave but the baker now held the bun to his nose, staring so intently at it that Tabar wondered if he'd heard him at all.

The baker smoothed his fingertips over its crusty dome and sobbed the big, wailing cries of a small child, devastated, inconsolable. "Oh... the crust is burnt. Look how the crust is burnt."

Tabar dropped to the baker's side and took the man's hands in his, turning the bun this way and that. "See, there are only some small places. We can pick them off." One piece at a time they removed the char together until the baker smiled through his tears.

"It's gone! It's gone." He sat up, sniffed, and wiped his face along his sleeve, his eyes brimming with delight.

"Yes, the burnt parts are gone."

"No, it's gone... it's gone. Gone." The baker was somber again and Tabar wondered if this was the lightning Hordle had spoken of.

"Gone?"

The baker's hands latched onto Tabar's forearm, the surprise and certainty of the movement highlighting the clarity in the old man's eyes. "*She's* gone."

Tabar nodded once.

The old man copied his nod, a smile crossed his lips, and he released Tabar's arm. In the next breath, the baker grasped a bun and held it towards Tabar. "Fresh today... but we're all out of currants. You weren't quick enough for the currants! I baked these myself. How many for you?"

Tabar rose from the side of the pallet bed. "I'll take three, thank you, baker." He juggled the buns as the baker loaded them into his hands.

"I'll have more on the morrow. Be sure you're early if you want currants."

"Farewell, baker," Tabar said, but the baker was too busy rummaging among his blankets and mumbling about the price of currants to notice him leave the room.

T abar pulled his cap down against the rain. Of course it was raining. This was the road to Tun-

stream. The wind drove the rain sideways like a big
wet scythe working its way across the landscape,
sweeping across the road in front of him with a rhythm
of its own understanding. By the time the sun crept
from behind the clouds again Tabar's clothes clung
to his skin and his feet squelched in his boots. Kish
wouldn't be so foolish to walk in the rain. She would
have holed up somewhere and waited for the storm to
pass, and that's what he was counting on.

He almost despaired of finding her before nightfall.
The shadows lengthened and with them a new energy
flooded his legs. *Where was she? Was she safe?* Just
when he thought he couldn't run any longer, Tabar
spotted what he hoped was her form disappearing
beyond a rise.

He waved. "Kish!"

Kish turned and ran to greet him, stopping a few
paces from him and wringing her hands. His broad
smile offered forgiveness for her outburst and she
leapt into his arms and laughed. Kish took his hand
and led him to the rise.

"Look," she said, pointing to a group of houses in the
next dale. "I think that's Tunstream."

W ooden fences ran on either side of the road that
led into the village. Wildflowers with masses of
tiny white heads dotted its length and fields sloped
gently away, ending only in forest or the fertile marker
of a stream. The village appeared open, with houses
deliberately spaced apart, nothing like the crisscross
lanes of the village they'd left behind. As they drew
closer, Tabar tugged on his cap. His clothes were dry,

and the rain had washed him clean, yet he seemed to have trouble catching his breath. Would they send him away? Kish was magnificent, as always. She strode into the village, her eyes wide with wonder. Tabar decided right then that if they sent him away, knowing Kish was safe would be enough. It would always be enough.

A solid, middle-aged man with a light beard approached them and shook Tabar's hand.

"Is this Tunstream?" Kish asked before any introductions could be made.

"It is," the man replied and guided them from the path of a farm cart. "Hass," he said as he offered his hand to Kish, and to Tabar again.

Tabar noticed the man's eyes linger on his features. "It's only important that Kish here is safe. I didn't think to bring a cart."

"It doesn't matter how you got here," Hass said, "just that you *are* here."

"Will you be staying?" The woman's voice appeared before her body did. Her head bobbed until they reached an agreement about the late hour and then she left with a wave of her arm. "The old hut is ready for guests, Hass. I'll give it a quick tidy."

Hass led Tabar and Kish across the village square. He nodded at the other villagers on their way to the small shingled houses that surrounded it. This was unlike any other square Tabar and Kish had heard of. It held a large fire pit in its center with logs lying along each side. Tabar watched as men gathered near the logs and only noticed they'd arrived at the door of the hut when Kish nudged him.

"Here you are." Hass opened the door.

The one room contained a bed and a table, but the hearth immediately drew Tabar to its side. He ran his fingers along its stone edges and admired its practical design.

Kish looked out the tiny window at the fields in the dusky light and beamed at Tabar. "It's perfect." She then turned her attention back to Hass, who waited outside. "Tell me about Tunstream," she said as Tabar followed her to Hass's side.

No matter how much Tabar tried to follow Hass's words, the antics of the men trying to light the fire with wood still damp from the storm was too distracting.

Kish placed her hand on his arm. "Go on then, Magic Man."

Tabar turned to his host. "Would the men be offended if I offered to help them?"

"I doubt that very much." Hass laughed. "Look at them."

Hass and Kish watched Tabar introduce himself to the men by the fire pit. "So tell me," Hass said, "Why is he magic, or is that something I don't want to know?"

Kish smiled. "You just watch. He can set anything on fire."

It wasn't long before the men around the fire pit cheered and Hass smiled, nodded, and bowed to Kish.

Tabar sat on one of the logs alongside the fire pit and tended the fire as darkness approached. The log wasn't particularly comfortable, but his legs appreciated the rest and protested with aches each time he moved to check on the coals. Even though the shingled houses of Tunstream surrounded him, he could breathe. Tabar counted about twenty people, mostly adults, some half-grown children.

"Bring your supper," Hass called to the villagers that milled around the square, "We've new neighbors."

Before long, people eating meals of vegetables, bread, and broth filled the logs. Kish and Tabar gratefully received their own bowls filled to the brim.

Tabar pushed his spoon into the piping stew, and snuck a look at Kish under his cap. She smiled at him. Apart from some bakery bread with Kish, he had never shared a meal with anyone, let alone a whole village. He sat and watched as the villagers talked around the fire and stayed very still so as not to remind them he was there. When he looked around, as inconspicuously as he could, he couldn't see a sty anywhere. A farming discussion caught his attention and highlighted just how much he didn't understand. But he wanted to. Hass winked at his confused face and Tabar felt strange. *Safe.*

When the villagers and their discussions had worn themselves out for the night, Kish took Tabar's hand and led him to the little hut that was now their home.

5

As the moons passed, Tabar worked hard to make their home hospitable. He repaired the roof they didn't know leaked until a storm passed through, concentrated hard in the fields, and learned as much as he could. His agricultural knowledge had consisted of some of the widows' half-truths and things he'd discovered in their fields himself. Now he could ask questions any time, and about anything.

Before anyone really noticed, it became the village habit for Tabar to light and tend the nightly fire in the square. Each evening he made sure it was strong and well stoked before nightfall gathered the villagers together.

"What is it with you and fire?" someone asked Tabar. He looked at the scars on his arms and remembered fear and torture, but also how fire had saved him in the widows' cottage and how it had brought Kish to him. He shrugged.

Hass chuckled as he walked past. "Magic with the fire, and magic in the field," he said. Tabar couldn't imagine that his work bumbling with the scythe and bouncing a plow around the earth was any form of magic. He laughed when he realized Hass spoke in jest.

Just that afternoon Tabar led the horse to plow channels in the fallow ground and the harsh earth had pushed the plow off line.

"Tabar! Whoa!" Hass had shouted and showed him where his line didn't follow the previous channel.

"Surely it won't make that much difference?" Tabar said. It was hot, and the men were already tired.

"Up here it doesn't, but down there it will." Hass pointed further down the field. "Let's get back to where we went off track."

Tabar tried not to take the complaints of the men personally, and Hass used his lesson as a refresher for the others. "Men, I know it's frustrating, but you've got to be prepared to go back and repeat things and do things that aren't pleasant to find out where you went off track. It's better in the long run. Better for your future. How do you want your future to look? That's what you've got to ask yourself. How do you want your harvest to look?"

At that moment, with perspiration trailing into his eyes, Tabar was convinced Hass was a pedantic bully. He also knew Hass was right, and he loved learning from him. The other men seemed to love him too, and although there was an occasional grumble, there was never any ill feeling between them.

Tabar rubbed on the top of his cap. The only thing he missed about working alone in the fields was not wearing his cap, particularly on hot afternoons like that one. His scalp prickled in the heat and itched under it, yet he was happy to never remove it again if it meant he could stay in Tunstream.

After he'd re-plowed the line, he led the horse back to the men who waited by the water barrel with drinks in hand.

"Hot day," one said and scooped a ladle of water for him.

Tabar used the back of his hand to wipe the sweat from his brow. "Thanks." The motion collected the edge of his cap, and with reflexes as tired as his body, there was nothing Tabar could do but watch it tumble to the ground. He stared at it for a while where it sat awkwardly among the dust and stubble then reached down to collect it.

It had finally happened.

He was found and he couldn't bring himself to look at the men. The only sound was the breeze that crossed his ears as he waited what seemed like forever for their orders.

Hass broke the silence and dipped the ladle in the barrel for more water. "Bet it's cooler with that hat off, isn't it?"

"There's a nice breeze today," another noted.

Hass laughed and ruffled Tabar's hair, and Tabar felt something lift from the space above his head. He tilted his head and squinted against the sun, and the sudden lightness felt so real he looked for whatever it was floating up into the sky.

E ach night, after the evening meal, the conversations around the fire pit began. The villagers talked about the fields and the weather, and when everyone was relaxed and open, they mentioned any problems they might be having. Tabar waited for people to raise their voices but it didn't happen. He listened as everyone worked together to solve the problem. No one blamed the man who admitted he felt lazy and resentful; they helped him clarify why it might be, and worked on restoring him. Tabar learned new words, new ways of explaining things, and remembered to save his dumbest questions for Hass when they worked in the fields.

Kish thrived around Tunstream's fire, and if he didn't love her to bursting when she was six summers old and fighting with the adults in the bakery, he loved her more in the firelight as she discussed—still sometimes heatedly—the policies of the Hall. She nodded in understanding when someone showed her a new way, and the villagers listened carefully to even her most absurd plans. She blossomed right in front of him, and her anger and defensiveness softened ... a little. He wondered if Kish was right after all, that one person's determined choice and purpose might change all their futures.

T abar entered the hut and grabbed one of the small loaves of bread from the table. Kish snatched it back from him and handed him a thick crust. "They're for the fire tonight. Have you started it yet?"

Tabar pinched at the crust and chewed. "Just about to. I saw you from the fields today. You were out walking on the road."

"You were watching me?"

"How can I not?"

Kish broke open a loaf and showed him inside. "I went to look for herbs for the bread. Maya joined me."

"The old lady? I thought that was her. Hard to tell from that distance. A woman dressed in a pile of rags with skinny legs...can't really see those features from the field."

"She's amazing!"

"I'm sure she is." Tabar scanned the table for something to tide his hunger over until supper, but there were only the untouchable full loaves or pieces of herbs.

"She knows so much! She taught me about yarrow." Kish handed him a stalky sprig of green with a mass of tiny white flowers at its head.

Tabar twirled it in his fingers. "And what about yarrow?"

"It heals everything."

"Everything?"

"All right, well, maybe not *everything*, but it's good for almost any affliction." Kish counted on her fingers. "Bleeding, breathing, afflictions of the skin, heat in the body; it heals everything!"

Tabar raised his eyebrows.

"I hope she joins me again tomorrow,"

"Why don't you ask her?"

"I couldn't do that. She's so wise and almost . . . I don't know . . . regal,"

"An old woman wearing rags is regal?"

Kish stared out her little window into the fields. "I want to be like her one day."

"You want to be like someone else?" Tabar wondered what the village had done to the Kish he knew.

"She knows everything, she's so passionate, so solid. .. but she doesn't yell like I do—I mean—used to."

Tabar wasn't sure what he thought about this new Kish. This softened version. He loved that she didn't need to defend herself anymore, but he also knew no one had ever impressed her. In his wildest dreams he'd never imagined an old quiet medicine woman with skinny legs and wild hair would be the one to sway Kish.

"Passionate *and* quiet?" Tabar repeated and wondered if such a thing was possible for her.

"Yes. And dignified and sure of herself. She knows what to say, and when, and also... *how* to say it."

"I see," Tabar said, and watched the yarrow twirl as he rolled its stalk between his fingers. "And this knowing when to speak and when not to... that must balance somewhere between bravery and stupidity."

Kish placed the loaves onto a tray and handed it to Tabar. "Maybe only time will tell which one I am."

"I have a feeling that stupid people *think* they can change the world, but it's the brave ones that actually do it." Tabar kissed her forehead and carried the tray of loaves to the door.

"So you think I'm one of the brave ones?" she called after him.

"I know you are."

The evening meal had only finished, and Old Sol, the village chandler, leaned sideways and slumped off the edge of the log.

"At least he ate some food this time," a villager said.

"At a ratio to five parts ale," another added.

People around the fire smiled, but no one laughed. "Go gently, his wife's only been passed a week."

Grief still sat heavily on the whole village and Tabar couldn't bring himself to imagine what life without Kish would be like. Hass nodded to him and they both rose to collect Old Sol and get him to his feet.

"Off to your cot with you now, time for some sleep," Hass said, lifting Sol gently.

"I'm hiding," he slurred, "and I can hide wherever I want."

"Yes, you can hide, and when you're sick of hiding, we'll be here waiting for you." Hass draped one of Sol's arms across his shoulder and Tabar bent and slipped under the other.

Tabar pushed Sol's door open. "The quickest way to come out of hiding, Sol, is to know that's what you're doing. I'd say you're almost there."

"Yeah, but I won't remember any of this in the morning," Sol assured them as he fell into his bed.

"But your heart will, Sol," Hass said as they left and closed the door.

After they'd settled him and returned, the fire burned bright and hot. Meals sat delightfully in the villager's bellies and along with laughter, they toasted each other's goodness.

Hass strolled from one side of the gathering to the other, stopping to comment and toast with others along the way. Without even pausing his conversation, Hass removed Tabar's cap and dropped it into his lap as he passed him. The villagers toasted, swigged, and laughed.

Hass prepared to seat himself on the other side of the fire but first raised his cup. "And tonight we will hear from Tabar."

The villagers raised their cups and cheered.

"We will?" Tabar asked.

Hass eyed him sternly through the fire. "We will."

Each man and woman had brought their thoughts, understandings, and lessons to the fire, but what could Tabar contribute? He knew nothing about politics, or market forces, or justice. He *hated* history. The only thing Tabar knew anything about was fire. How could anything he said about fire be important enough to bring to the whole village? He thought about all the different things he'd learned about lighting a fire. That was where a fire started; its birth. Instead, he decided he'd tell them about the life of the fire.

Tabar stood and rolled up his sleeves so the villagers could see his scars. "Once, fire only brought me terror," he began. He placed a hand on Kish's shoulder. "Then it brought me love. Then it brought me here. I'd like to tell you what I've learned from fire, and in particular, *this* fire."

The villagers turned their faces from Tabar and peered into the fire, wondering what Tabar had found in there they hadn't.

"All wood burns the same," Tabar said. "It's only the bark on the outside that is any different. Now, catching different woods alight, that's what takes skill, patience, and determination. But once the bark has burned away, there's only the inner left to burn, regardless of what tree it came from."

Tabar moved and looked at the fire from each angle. "This fire has burned for a while; you can all see how the coals have formed and how they glow. Notice how they're all the same rich color, and when fanned, they flare again, changing color as one, even though these logs were originally from different trees." Tabar used a stick to point at the fire. "See the coals there on the outside, the cooler ones? It's only when they move away from the source and start to cool down that you see the fissures and cracks that set them apart as different from the others. When a log is left alone to gather the heat, it forms coals and glows, but when you shuffle it around and never let it be still . . ." Tabar used the stick to push the logs and move some coals to the edges of the fire, ". . . you make a pretty show of sparks, but not much else."

Tabar fanned the coals, and the villagers leaned back from the heat. "When the coals glow hot, any difference among them disappears. Every coal is the same in its function and its potential to burn bright. They don't fight the fire; they follow the natural progression, they burn, they glow, and they blend and become one. See how it looks like they have no edges, as if the coals are about to melt into each other? There's only one color, one force, and it's not even the flame. The flame is what we focus on when we think of fire, but it's the coals from deep inside that's the source of its power."

Hass nodded slowly as if he was deep in thought. "That's all well and good, Tabar, but how does your lesson apply to Tunstream?"

Tabar walked the short distance to his hut and returned with a piece of firewood from his hearth.

He dropped the wood gently into the fire and a puff of sparks pushed into the air. "When I place this wood here, from my own home, I do so knowing what it is to be open and honest and safe with another. This fire is something I've never seen before, something I've never known before. Tunstream burns away the outside layers, it disregards them to get to the core of the matter. I see it when we work to solve the same problem, when we turn to coals and work as one. That's where Tunstream's real power is, in the coals, in its intention. Of course, a man can stand alone in his purpose and withstand a fire, but when another stands beside him, like you've shown me here in Tunstream, the fire grows hotter, consumes them and their differences, and they become coals all made of the same power, and things can truly change."

Hass coughed, rose from the log, and walked away from the fire. No one spoke. Perhaps Tabar's observations weren't helpful to Tunstream at all. The villagers watched Hass lumber to his nearby home then return and stand at Tabar's side.

Hass produced a small log from behind his back and slammed it into the fire. Sparks rained down and he slapped Tabar's back and toasted him. "A man might be called to the fire, but it's when there's no bark that no man is alone. Welcome to Tunstream!"

The villagers continued their toasts and brought wood from their own hearths and added it to the fire with words about coals and power. Tabar's favorite was something about how they always had the power to choose to let the bark burn away and get the work done. They all stayed together and watched as the bark burned to ashes on the new wood and the coals became one.

6

I t was cold, early dawn when Tabar banged on the
door of Maya's house. Her husband greeted him,
his hair as puffy as a dandelion. He knew straight away;
he didn't have to ask why Tabar huffed and puffed in
the half light. "It's time, Maya, quickly."

Maya was at the door moments later and brushed
her way past Tabar with a small but encouraging smile.

Back in their hut, Kish smiled and squeezed his
hand. "I'll be fine. Maya's here now."

Tabar paced around the square trailed by a line of
men offering their support. He tried his hardest not
to worry but felt like he didn't draw breath while he
waited. After an eternity, the door of his hut opened
and Maya beckoned him inside.

If Tabar thought his heart felt like it would burst
with Tunstream's kindness and acceptance, it rup-
tured into a thousand pieces the day his son was born.
The sight of the two most precious beings on his earth
safe was more relief than he could handle, and he
rested against the doorframe as silky gratitude flooded
him from head to toe.

The villagers gathered and murmured outside the
hut. Tabar heard their calls of, "Have you checked?"
"Maya, have you checked?" but the voices brushed

over him while he stood transfixed at the vision of Kish holding their child.

Maya moved to go outside. "I'll answer for you," she said to Kish. "I'll be back with some broth."

As soon as Maya left, Tabar went straight to Kish's side. His son, wrapped in soft cloth, lay nestled in the crook of her arm. "What a life I am living. An unwanted piglet with a castle of my own."

Kish took his hand and squeezed it gently. "There will be no more talk of piglets, do you understand?"

Tabar nodded, and she lifted his hand and stroked it over the head of his fair-haired son. "Would you look at that hair?" he said.

"He's like a sprig of yarrow under our roof."

"We will make it true, I promise."

"What?"

"That yarrow heals everything."

Tabar looked back to the door. "What do they want checked?"

"His eyes."

"Eyes?"

"For the Eariss."

Tabar frowned at her.

"We're all waiting for the one the legends say will bring about change."

"And you think it's him? Was it him?"

Kish shook her head. "Not according to the legends." She sighed and rested so heavily into the pillow that Tabar bit back his questions and simply kissed her forehead.

"Sleep, *ma-kish*," he whispered.

He built them a fire, a red-hot glowing protector that sealed the moment in their minds forever.

The candlelight flickered gently against the walls of the hut and their baby boy murmured and moved in his sleep. Tabar got up once again to check him and Kish pulled him back by his nightshirt. "He'll be sure to let us know when he needs us."

Tabar adjusted Kish's blankets and pillows instead. "You've slept well? You're comfortable?"

She nodded and patted the bed next to her.

Tabar relented. "I've been thinking about your Eariss legend," he said as he lay gently beside her. "I even asked in the village about it. They said that in the fable it is told the Eariss would be born of fire with rainbows in their eyes and raise an army to sweep in a new way, but the road to the new way wasn't pleasant." Kish confirmed his words with a nod. "Explain to me how you're always looking to the future and change and yet when something as important as the birth of your child happens, the whole village reverts to fables and legends?"

"That's because the legends are about change. If you listen behind the stories of flames, color, and flower, it's all about change." Kish took a deep breath, closed her eyes, and smiled. "I love it. I love its possibility and it runs in my veins and in my father's, and in his father's before him. It's in all of us."

Tabar lay still for a moment and tried to feel what was in his veins. Nothing much but tiredness and overwhelming love for Kish and their son.

She stroked his arm. "That's what the Eariss is, *hope*. The tales are hope. A sign not unlike a labor pain. You know birth is imminent, and there will be pain. Things break in pain to bring forth something new. The soil breaks for the seed. If you fought the soil breaking, how would your crops ever grow?"

The baby murmured again and Tabar rose before Kish could stop him. She spoke as Tabar watched him sleep. "Your son."

"My son."

"You believe he can do anything?"

"Of course."

"He can change the world?"

Tabar smiled. "If he's anything like his mother then it's inevitable, isn't it?"

I nsects buzzed and the whole field took on a golden glow in the afternoon light. Without letting go of the ties in his hand, Tabar managed to wipe his brow with his upper arm and still secure the pile of sheaves at his feet. A short distance away, Hass finished tying the last of his section and stood to stretch his back. He nodded toward the water barrel. "A drink first, before we finish."

It had been a long season, and not just because it was Tabar's first in a large field. Everyone seemed tired. Water breaks stretched out the day but also cushioned them against exhaustion. With only himself and Hass at the water barrel, Tabar took the opportunity to speak.

"Can I ask about your talk at the fire last night?"

"As always, Tabar."

"The guards. From Brennyn Hall. What did you call it? Collection, subscription?"

"Conscription."

Tabar swallowed some water and nodded. "That's it. How's it work?"

"The Hall needs manpower to enforce its laws, but it also needs the villages and farmers to provide. So what they do is take able-bodied men and force them to serve time as guards."

"What if they don't want to?"

"No choice, I'm afraid."

Tabar had only met one guard in his life. Any time a guard turned up in the old village, the widows would relegate Tabar to the sty. "They should just use Trothsmen, then" he said.

"Not enough of those heartless bastards to cover the land."

Tabar had never met a Trothsman, but he'd heard about them from Kish and the stories she heard from travelers in the bakery. Men as hard as their black leather armor; some said they were soulless, but Tabar wasn't sure that was possible. The only thing all the tales were certain of was that the men always did the Hall's bidding. Without fail. No matter how gruesome. Tabar usually imagined them sitting upon their black steeds coolly deciding who lived or died, oblivious to anything but their duty. The thought always made the pit of his stomach cold.

Hass broke his thoughts. "What worries you?"

"Will they come here . . . for us?" Tabar's wrists suddenly tingled with the sensation of ropes. "Will I be found?"

Hass stepped back and sized Tabar up. "The value of your strength would outshine any interest they may have in your origin. Besides, we're small...maybe they'll leave us alone. To make a unit of us, they'd have to take all the able-bodied men in the village. Best to get their men from the bigger towns and villages."

This satisfied Tabar. Surely the Hall wasn't so short-sighted to incapacitate an entire village when they had so many others to choose from. The more he thought about it, the more Hass's words made sense. They walked together to the far end of the field and planned to work their way back to the village as they collected and tied the final sheaves. Tabar counted how many of the sheaves were already the Hall's and shook his head. They wouldn't come here.

By the time they'd worked their way halfway up the field, Tabar and Hass had devised a system that eased their aching hands. One would squeeze the sheaf tightly while the other would apply the final binding and lift it onto the cart.

"It feels like we're making faster progress this way," Tabar said, lifting another sheaf high.

"Can't be sure it's quicker than working on our own sections, but it's definitely easier."

Tabar bent over the next sheaf and squeezed the stalks together. Hass's hands looped the tie around the stalks, once, twi –

Tabar's gaze shifted from Hass's hands to the way the man's eyes narrowed at something over Tabar's shoulder.

Tabar squinted. "What?"

"Nothing. Head down, Tabar," Hass said and busied his hands with the ties.

Tabar turned, but only caught a glimpse of the man and his jagged run into the forest. It was all he needed. The bedraggled uniform and the panicked way he checked behind him told Tabar all he needed to know.

"Turn away, Tabar," Hass said. "You saw a blur in the forest, nothing else." This time Tabar narrowed his eyes at Hass, who concentrated on the tie. "What we don't see, we can't tell."

"You want me to pretend I don't see a Brennyn guard running for his life?"

"That's exactly what I'm telling you."

Tabar looked toward the forest and remembered all the times he wanted to run from the widows. The man was no doubt terrified because he had no idea what would happen and whether he'd made the right decision. "Wouldn't it be better if he'd just stayed and did as he was told?"

"Not always," Hass said as he tied the last of the grain. "Sometimes it's just easier not to see."

Tabar understood but couldn't shake the heaviness that settled over them. "Just don't try telling Kish that!"

They laughed, and Tabar wondered what it was he was supposed to see now. As a child, he pretended he didn't see many things. What could he do back then, anyway? But now he was a man, and he felt it was time to do away with childish excuses. What was easy wasn't always right. Now he sounded like Kish. Did he have that inner obligation that Kish spoke of? The one that caused her so much joy but also so much pain? And did he even want it?

7

The crops were almost in, and dust and chaff blew about in the warm morning wind, forming little columns that danced along the lanes. In the little hut, Tabar, already dressed and ready for the fields, chose a log from his own hearth to add to the celebratory fire that night.

"This one, I think."

"I'm glad you started that fire tradition," Kish said as she worked some dough at the table. "So, it's the last of the winter wheat today?" she asked.

He kissed her cheek. "Hope so, then we'll finally get to celebrate."

Their son gurgled and crawled across the floor toward them, and Tabar greeted him with a sweep of his arm. "And you, my Yarrow, shall have some candied apple."

"Perhaps now he's a bit older we should start calling him by his real name?"

Tabar waved her concerns away. "Everyone knows him as Yarrow, the most loved and spoiled baby in Tunstream."

"That's because he's the only baby in Tunstream."

Tabar picked Yarrow up and planted kisses all down his neck, making the baby squeal with delight. Next he kissed Kish goodbye, then Yarrow, then Kish again.

"Off you go then," Kish said, pushing him out the door. "Finish the field, then you can have kisses."

"And candied apple?"

She sighed. "And candied apple."

T he men worked the fields, a new lightness in their gait and an expectation of satisfaction in the air.

"Is your Giselle making that spiced ale for tonight's fire?" one asked.

A pronounced nod brought about banter and commentary about previous encounters with her ale. "Just don't have as much as last time," someone said.

At first the noise seemed like a faint distraction, and Tabar might have thought it was thunder if the sky wasn't so clear. But as it grew louder, the men stopped their work and caught each other's glances, listening to the sound on the wind. One by one their agitation grew as though something tense spread among them, yet no one seemed to know what it was. A cloud of dust and blackness emerged from the forest road and pounded its way toward the village. The sound of so many hooves, urged on by shouts of Trothsmen, thudded into Tabar's ears and dried his throat. He didn't even realize he ran with the men across the field toward the village until his lungs were burning and his voice hoarse.

Yarrow!

The men were drawn like magnets even though they knew they headed into danger. Trothsmen dismounted and seized them as they entered the village square, shuffling and sorting them into groups while the men called to each other and their families. They lined

Tabar up with the other men along one side of the square and discarded the elderly into its center. The old men wandered to a log and sat shaking their gray heads in their hands. Energy crackled through Tabar's veins. He would run the moment he got a chance, just like the guard he saw in the forest. He turned his head to stare at Hass further down the line. Betrayal and rage simmered among all the men and added a layer of emotion underneath his own. Kish stood guarded by Trothsmen with the women and children on the opposite side of the square. Tabar hadn't told her about the runner; Hass said there was no need. Now they faced a situation they hadn't even discussed.

A villager pointed to the women and demanded an answer from the Trothsmen. "Why do you line the women and children up?"

Tabar had reeled over the intrusion into the village and the surrounding chaos, but now he noticed too. The men stopped their jostling, shocked.

A mounted Trothsman wheeled his horse around the square, sneering at their little village. "Welcome to the Brennyn Guards," he said, turning his head to ensure everyone heard his words. Tabar felt the coldness grow in his stomach as Trothsmen moved their horses to block the road. Others dismounted and stood guard over the men, as cold and black as he'd imagined them. "Your service begins this day."

Tabar already knew there was no way out. He searched for Kish in the line and found her clutching Yarrow in his sling, close to her chest. Her hands tugged at the fabric, adjusting it to cover his hair. Soon the Trothsman would finish his speech about their service and she could return to the hut. He waited to hear how long their service would be, prepared to calculate how many seasons would pass and whether the village could survive that long without them.

The mounted Trothsman walked his horse along the line of women as if inspecting troops and spoke as he rounded to face the men again. "The Hall has taken liberties," he began, a smile creeping across his face, "to ensure your continued loyalty and diligence."

Liberties?

The Trothsman continued, "Your families will be held for the duration of your service."

"Held?" a villager shouted. "Held where?" But the Trothsman ignored him and nodded an instruction to one of his kind who stood at the line of women. The man began to inspect the women, carefully, one at a time. Tabar quickly convinced himself they were checking for injuries and health; he couldn't bear the thought of any other categorization.

What would they do to Kish?

And she to them?

What if the old lady in the bakery was right; what if her mouth ended up being the death of her?

The inspecting Trothsman moved down the line closer to Kish. She pulled the sling closer. Tabar could tell by her stance that her jaw muscles twitched.

"Yarrow..." Tabar's voice was dry and cracked and his words came out as a whisper.

Maya burst through the line of Trothsmen, her frail frame covered in blankets from each home. She danced in front of the Trothsmen and swirled blankets like a mad woman.

"What is she *doing?*" a villager muttered under his breath. "Cursed Stars, not now Maya!"

Her husband followed her and pleaded with his wife to stop.

"Blankets for you," she said, and surprised everyone with her strength as a blanket landed over the mounted Trothsman. Maya threw blankets all around and screeched like a lunatic, her gray hair wild and unkempt.

The mounted Trothsman threw the blanket to the ground. "Get this mad woman away from us!"

At that, Maya stopped and appeared to gather her thoughts, and shook her head as if she'd just woken from a dream. "So you're not here for the blankets then? Are you sure? They're very good blank—"

"No!" the Trothsman boomed and pushed his horse forward. Tabar gasped as its hooves almost trampled her.

Maya wandered back to her home, a huge pile of blankets with little skinny legs walking out the bottom. Her husband followed, wringing his hands and collecting blankets as they fell from her pile.

Tabar returned his attention to Kish. She looked elegant among the madness, her neck stretched high, her eyes focused straight ahead, with their son nowhere to be seen.

The mounted Trothsman spoke again but Tabar couldn't hear anything. His eyes were fixed on Kish, and the sounds of his heartbeat consumed his senses. Kish lunged forward and the women around her grabbed her and pulled her back. One raised a finger to her lips and nodded at Kish.

The men were turned and marched away, flanked by Trothsmen's horses. Tabar caught his last glimpse of Kish as she stood tall, the muscles around her jawline tense as blood trickled from the corner of her mouth.

I t was two full days' march to Brennyn Hall. The tall gates swung open to a large stoned courtyard and Trothsmen escorted the men to disused stables for the night. Unlike the previous night on the road, there was no campfire. The fire had been small, with the men only able to add sticks, but they turned to coals just the same. The stable was cold and their only meal too light for their famished stomachs. Tabar lay on the cold stone and just like the previous night, wondered if someone had lit a fire for Kish, and if Yarrow cried out for him.

8

The next morning the men traded their field clothes for the guard's uniform of a blue tunic with a leather sash that ran across their bodies. Tabar's fingers followed the opening cut into the sash. The sheath for the dagger was empty; the Trothsmen weren't that stupid. Once dressed, the villagers surveyed each other, but no one had energy for expressions. Tabar blinked hard and wondered if the others had to make as much effort to see farmers in front of them and not uniforms.

"Put your back into it, ya lazy—"

Trothsmen swung clubs from their steeds when they deemed a villager unenthusiastic about their training. At day's end, the men dragged the unconscious—and no longer rebellious—from the fields that surrounded the Hall back into the stable. It only took a few weeks for their hunger and grief to crave the physical outlet the training fields provided.

"Hey, you!" a Trothsman called and pointed to a villager who stood at the edge of a practice bout. "Don't you run." He chuckled and turned to another villager. "He runs... your families die. Must've forgotten our agreement."

Tabar's feet were charged with energy; he wanted to run. He *needed* to run, to find Kish and Yarrow and keep running. But their lives now lay in the hands of these other villagers, the ones whose eyes he avoided for fear of accusation.

"I wasn't going to run!" the villager pleaded, and a pummel of fists brought him down and made sure no one else considered running. No one.

By the time their training introduced them to weapons, the villagers had forgotten to use them against the Trothsmen. They were too focused on the skills they'd developed in bloodied battles with each other, urged on by the Trothsmen's reminders of what might be happening to their families. Graphic details that riled the men to a sudden windstorm of emotion where no man had a foothold on anything, not even in their dreams.

When the men were assigned orders and set free to patrol and punish according to the laws of the Hall, they didn't need a Trothsman as chaperon, they had become their own troop of horror. Tabar watched the threshold of the Hall pass overhead as they marched out to do its bidding. His teeth were clenched and his body tight. He had not lit a fire in all that time.

I t started simply enough, with angry sneers and threats to anyone who dared mock them and the uniform they wore. Shoves quickly progressed to savage swings that left the impudent person sprawled on the floor of the tavern, workshop, marketplace, or wherever the troop considered themselves offended. When they'd run out of commoners to attack they always had each other. Each fix was stronger than the other, dulling their frustration, if just for a moment.

Like strong ale, violence softened the dagger blades that rested in their hearts. The daggers sat inside Tabar like a bubbling pot over a tavern's fire; always under pressure, watching and waiting for a chance to overflow.

"Did ya see the way he just looked at you, Tabar?" Hass slurred and stood in the dark tavern. "No respect, I say!" He pointed his tankard accusingly toward a farmer who dropped his gaze. The farmer eased his ale onto the table and edged toward the door. Tabar was already standing, his troop members slapping his back. "Off you go," they cried. "This one's all yours."

It had been another long day and the simmering pot inside Tabar was bubbling at the edges. He charged through the doorway and tackled the farmer to the ground within a few strides. The slight farmer was no match for Tabar's strength, and he raised his arms to protect himself as Tabar flipped him to his back and cracked his fist into the man's eye socket.

The suppressed rage erupted and spread like acid through his senses. Tabar's fists plowed into the man, harder and faster, each blow removing a blade from within his chest. He was active, powerful, fighting against the pain, not sitting around absorbing it. Tabar roared and slammed his fist into the man's bloodied face. Then again, harder. Power surged through his body, collected the pain, and transformed it to nothingness the moment it entered another. What alchemy! What magic was this? This was a different kind of magic. He didn't even have to know what to do. It just came and swept him away from himself.

In his frenzy, he hadn't noticed the men lock their arms under his and drag him from the farmer's limp body. Tabar panted in exhilaration and fought their hold. He needed more. It didn't matter what took the pain away, or for how long, only that it went.

There was other magic too. Like when Tabar saw himself in those they beat as if he'd somehow possessed the bodies of the older boys in Lewtshire all those summers ago. Now it was him laughing at another's pain. Strangely, he understood their laughing faces and compulsion now, but didn't understand himself. He was doing things he vowed he would never do. And how was it possible to feel so much power yet feel so helpless at the same time? The violence kept those questions at bay too.

On the longer walks between remote villages when his mind was free to wander, he deliberately pushed his memories of Kish aside. They crushed his chest, and he was too ashamed to even imagine her face. Everyone else walked those stretches in silence too. There wasn't anything to say.

Yarrow grew wild there, in fields and along the edges of the road.

Everyone saw it, but no one acknowledged it.

Tabar didn't even want to touch it.

The troop followed Hass off the road as the light faded. It was another habit that arrived among them unannounced and unquestioned. Once he'd decided on a satisfactory spot for their camp Hass pointed to a clearing on the ground. "Get to it, Magic Man."

Magic Man.

Those words were the closest anyone came to mentioning Tunstream, or anything that existed before they marched out the Hall gates dressed in blue. Tabar felt it too; their lack of choice was so heavy it seemed impossible to carry the weight of memories as well.

Tabar gathered and arranged the kindling. Instinct told him something was amiss in its structure; he studied it and then rearranged the pattern of laid twigs and branches to best account for the breeze. He considered his re-formed campfire and then lifted his eyes to the men working around him. They prepared food, argued, and cleared the camp area for sleep.

How could any of them have known what the shock of their service and training would do to them? It had fired their reflexes and instincts, but their behavior was beyond that now. They were making choices. *Sometimes it's easier not to see.* Would Hass have ever thought his words would apply to their own behavior?

Tabar coaxed a small flame to life and fed it dried moss and leaves. It licked its way around the twigs, grew stronger, and made a bold attack on a split branch. Tiny sparks signaled its advance inward and Tabar imagined the fragmented coals that would appear in its place. In Tunstream, the men would have faced their reactions and understood them. Showed compassion for each other and worked together to find a solution. Tabar ducked and covered his head as dust, sticks, and flame flew about his face and two scuffling guards cursed and shoved each other through the fire. They tumbled off into the woods followed by several of their laughing and cursing comrades.

Tabar gathered the pieces and re-formed the fire, including the new sticks he discovered. Using the old to create the new; he'd heard something like that before. He nodded to himself. He was re-forming it to work again... and he was *choosing* how to do it.

The men had a choice too, and the ability to change the structure of how they were dealing with what was around them, and what was inside them.

Why not start with a choice about how they spent their time around the fire? They could spend it drinking themselves to oblivion and fighting or returning to the honesty and trust they found around Tunstream's fire.

Was it worth explaining it to them, daring to call the pain to the surface?

Was it worth a beating, or worse?

Tabar rose next to the fire. "If we all get a log...," he said. But then men shouted him down.

"Don't want to hear it, just start the damn fire, Tabar."

"We only need its warmth."

"Enough with the nonsense."

"More ale over here."

Tabar stoked the fire, jabbed at it, and sent sparks into the air. He spent the night like he spent most others, drunk and shuffling the coals around, making sure they didn't sit still for too long.

9

It was just a regular night. The usual agitation sat over their camp and Tabar took the opportunity to relieve himself not only physically, but to take some time away from the others. He kicked at the branch that blocked his path through the grove and ignored the guard's calls that he left the fire unattended. Just let one of them try to accuse him of running! Couldn't a man even take a leak in peace?

He wobbled on the uneven ground that surrounded the trees, crossed the road, and staggered headlong into a tree. His hand slapped onto its smooth bark. *This'll do.* The stars swayed in the treetops while he attended to himself, so he carefully brought his head level.

What was that moving on the road?

Tabar stood in the center of the road and waited for the shape to reach him, turning his head and trying to focus on it in the darkness. A grin stretched across his face.

What luck.

An idler.

This was one smaller than the usual bawdy enter-tainers they'd meet along the road. They were always good for a tale or a song, or some of that strange juggling that Tabar could never master. When they were done, they'd pay them well, or beat them. Who was he kidding? It was usually a beating. It kept with their entertainment theme.

The brainless idler nearly walked right into him.

He laughed and grabbed its arm, delighted to be bringing some form of distraction to camp. This one didn't fight as much as the others and Tabar thrust it in front of the men as if he'd just returned from a hunt.

He expected cheers at his delivery but for a moment there was no sound, only the cracks of the fire as the men looked up from their meals. The idler's traveling robe had come loose and sat in a pile near the fire. A young woman dressed in men's clothes stood before them.

Who'd ever heard of a girl idler? His stomach seized as if an invisible fist had laid a blow there. Cold horror spread through his body, —and he'd just thrown her straight into the guard's hands.

"It's her!" a voice said as the men rose to their feet as one.

"The one that escaped from the Hall."

"Fancy getting orders to hunt this wench and she comes to us."

The men laughed as if they'd just discovered some great fortune but surged toward her as if the hunt was still on.

Tabar launched himself at them.

He swung at them and them at him, shouting and screaming more with panic than rage. Latching onto their arms, he pulled them from her, and some he took by the hair and flung to nearby trees. He leapt onto Hass's back and hung around his neck while Hass growled and tried to shake him off. When Tabar's grip failed and he dropped to his feet, Hass turned and shoved him so hard he landed on his back. Hass raised a large, gleaming log from the fire above Tabar's head, slurring and spitting his hatred at him. "Stay away from me, you filthy dreg!" Tiny dots of coal glowed at the end of the log, and then it smoked and was gone.

At that moment the camp lit up with lights, but not like candles or any other light Tabar had ever seen. They were swirling colors that whipped around the camp. How was it possible to *feel* lights? What was in that ale? And how could it be coming from the girl? The men froze where they stood, sat, and lay.

"Arco Eariss," one mumbled, and the others cursed. *Eariss*... wasn't that one of Kish's strange beliefs? Fire and lights, she'd said. Tabar's skin tingled with gooseflesh. He frowned through the lights as they died down, his head still swaying and his heart thumping. The guards retreated as far from her limp and naked body as they could.

"What do we do with it?" someone asked Hass.

"If the Hall wasn't so obsessed with this trollop, we wouldn't be in this mess."

"Well, go on then, kill her."

"I'm not going anywhere near that thing."

"Scared of a girl?"

"That's not a girl."

"What is it then?"

They answered him with jugs of ale. "Drink up, there's a cold night ahead." They drank until there were no more thoughts of lights, or pain, or Tunstream, or the Eariss. Tabar counted them as they passed out one by one.

W as the world swaying, or was it him? Him. It was always him. Tabar sat on a log as the girl's form shivered in the moonlight, exposed and vulnerable. He couldn't fight against the visions of Kish's face; it was as if the ale invited them to torture him. Her face shone like it did when she talked of rainbow lights and hope. Tabar smashed his stick into the fire, watched the sparks float by his face, and emptied his jug once more.

The girl woke, and her cry forced his vision of Kish into the flames. Incapable of forming words, Tabar gave a low, guttural growl. His eyes scrunched up against a wave of heat from the fire and he returned to prodding the fire with the stick in his hand, sending sparks flying high into the air above the guard's camp.

She crawled around the campfire. *She won't last long out here.* That's what they'd said. *Let her go where she wants.* Tabar squeezed an eye shut to focus on the small lump at his feet. A doll. Made of straw and tied with string. He scrunched it in his hand and the hair stuffed inside it pushed it back into shape. It's something he might've made for Kish once upon a time. *Kish.*

The girl held her hand out for the doll, and anger pounded into his heart. Why doesn't she go back to the Hall? If it wasn't for her, he'd still be in Tunstream. If it wasn't for her, he wouldn't be here by a fire with Kish who knows where and his son without his mother.

"You want your doll?" Tabar thought he asked her the question but maybe he hadn't said it out loud. It didn't matter anyway. "You want something? Desperately?" He offered it to her and waited until he saw hope in her eyes before he tossed it in the fire. Her hope crumbled just like his did every night he had to start a fire without Kish. He felt some of his pain lift, just a fleeting moment, and the sudden lightness tickled him, and he laughed.

She wandered off into the dark and Tabar returned to stoking the fire and watching the sparks dance. He fought the unease that grew inside him. Why should he be generous when no one offered the same to him? She was highborn anyway. What would she know about survival? Tabar shuffled the coals, still not content to let them settle. The men had joked and belittled the lights and rainbows as they drank, but they trembled even as they laughed. He closed his eyes and tried to make sense of it. This was *their* legend... wasn't it supposed to run in their veins? It wasn't enough for the Hall to take them from Tunstream; it ruined their legends now too?

Wasn't that what they just witnessed—a legend?

Did they see it?

Of course they did, they *named* it.

Tabar wished he could ask Kish what this all meant. What would happen now? Would they be freed? How long would they have to wait to be together with their families again?

"Kish?" he said to the fire, hoping she'd explain it to him again. "Kish?" he called and didn't care that he was begging.

T abar knew they needed to do something... return somewhere, but his foggy brain couldn't place it. Hass snored, sprawled out on the ground, his hand now more comfortable around the handle of a jug than a plow. *The plow.* They needed to go back to where it went wrong and correct their course. They needed to return to what they'd created in Tunstream. Tabar stood up, lost his balance, and fell back to the log. He couldn't see where the girl had gone. Tunstream was the most powerful thing he had, and everything he had failed to offer the girl. Tabar tapped the stick on the log, not concerned about sparks anymore. He needed a plan. The men snored and rolled around the campfire. How could he get them back to Tunstream? He didn't share their history; Hass had made that perfectly clear, yet the urgent need to do something, *anything*, sat like a rock in the center of his body.

"Who am I to say anything?" he asked the fire. "Who am I to change anything? *Dreg!*"

*J*ust survive and get home.

Tabar nodded at his thought—it was easy.

Home to what? Tunstream wouldn't be the same again. And what would they be taking back to restart? Resilience or misery? Again, they had a choice. Tabar thought about the runner. Did he run under these conditions, driven mad by grief and worry, or was *his* run the reason for their circumstances? It was easy to blame him, to hate the faceless runner. Just as it was easier to blame the girl for reminding them of their hope. What they endured would either bond them or destroy them. If it destroyed them, it destroyed Tunstream.

Another fiery breeze brushed Tabar's cheek and his eyes closed as he swayed against the ale and what was left of his life. No matter how much he hated these men, he loved them. He would do anything for them, and they him. They were already doing it for each other, trapped in this torturous camaraderie.

The longer Tabar sat by the fire the more determined he grew that they would face what happened to them and develop the strength to survive it. Things would change even if they hurt, like the breaking soil. Tabar smiled when he imagined Kish's face. Something new was coming. He could feel it deep in his bones.

He looked around the campfire and shook his head. His men weren't even worthy of going home, but he would make sure they were. *His men.* When did they become his men? The moment he decided he would take these men made of wet wood and set them on fire.

※ ※ ※ ※ ※

"**D**o you know what fire does?" Tabar said to the men as they began to stir and wake up in the early morning.

"Not now, Tabar," someone grumbled, "for Stars sake,"

But Tabar spoke louder, a nighttime of thoughts finally receiving voice. "It burns the same wherever it is. In the village, in a bakery, in a hearth, here... in Tunstream." The men growled in response, some from their backs, others from their hands and knees on their way to standing. Tabar dodged a jug thrown in his direction. "I want to return to Tunstream."

"We all want to return, Tabar."

"No, I want to return to how we behaved at Tunstream before all of this, not the village, if it still exists. I'm talking about the Tunstream that's inside us,

buried under all our anger and regret and remorse...
and shame... and disgust." No one had dared to ac-
knowledge their behavior, let alone name it, and he
watched their fists clench and heard their puffs of
breath. "It's still there, I know it is."

"It's too late, Tabar. We can't go back."

"But we get to choose how we go forward. No one
took that away from us. We gave it up."

Hass shrugged, and Tabar pointed to him. "Hass.
The plow. You told me to go back to where you went
wrong and correct it."

"This is different."

"How do you want your future to look, Hass? Like
this?"

The men yelled obscenities. Some, including Hass,
picked up branches and charged themselves with the
energy needed to silence a foe. Tabar raised his voice
above them. "Is it easier not to see? Is that what you're
telling me, Hass? To not see ourselves?"

Tabar ducked the branch Hass swung at his head
but couldn't avoid the charge that slammed his back
into a tree. Hass shoved his forearm against Tabar's
neck. "Enough, Dreg!" he shouted, close enough that
his spittle landed on Tabar's face.

Tabar's blow to Hass's ribs sent them both tumbling
toward the fire. They landed beside it with a thud, the
cheers and jeers of the men ringing in Tabar's ears.

Hass appeared above Tabar, his knees digging into
Tabar's upper arms. Tabar swung his legs but couldn't
connect. Panic shot through his veins as other hands
grabbed his legs and held them down. Boots pinned
his open hands beside his head.

"Shut! Up! Dreg!" Hass shouted and reached to the
fire.

The stick wasn't that wide, perhaps a finger width, but its tip matched Hass's anger. Tabar thrashed as the stick hovered over his face before Hass pushed it into Tabar's exposed forearm. Tabar grunted and clenched his teeth.

"Hurt?"

His arm didn't hurt as much as he thought it would. It was his whole body that ached and felt as heavy as lead. Tabar didn't notice when the men fell silent and released him, only that they were no longer there.

Hass rose and shoved Tabar with his foot for good measure. "Good."

In that moment he understood Kish's passion. It was never about her voice, or her right to say something; it was about their right to hear it. When she fought, it wasn't for herself, it was for them and their ability to choose. Kish didn't fight people physically, but it was just as bloody. More than anything, though, he understood her drive. Tabar rose and threw himself onto Hass as he walked away. Hass turned and Tabar landed a blow to his jaw and received one in return.

"What are you doing?" Hass yelled.

"Trying to get you to listen."

Hass shoved him backwards into a tree and hit him again. "I don't need to listen to you."

Tabar tasted blood in his mouth. "You do. You can't see."

"I can see fine," he said, this time landing one on Tabar's cheekbone.

"That makes you feel better?"

Hass replied with another blow to his face, "Yes."

"But it doesn't get rid of it, does it? It just stops it for a while."

"A while is good enough."

"No, it's not. Not anymore!"

Hass held his fist near Tabar's face. They puffed and bled and Hass's eyes moved from rage to anger. Hass thrust his hand to Tabar's chest, scrunched his tunic in his fist and threw Tabar to the ground before striding away. The camp seemed silent as if the forest itself was waiting for the next move. Tabar lay still, out of ideas and devoid of energy.

"A while isn't good enough anymore. Not for me," one man said.

Others nodded and lowered their faces. Tabar closed his eyes and exhaled. The men had heard him, even if Hass hadn't.

Tabar used the back of his hand to wipe the blood from his mouth and face. The men seated around the fire waited for him to speak but he didn't even know what to say. The flames reminded him of their source.

"Remember the coals?" he said to the men. "Remember how we moved and worked as one?" He waited for nods and then continued. "These circumstances separated us, we tried to deal with it separately, and it created a barrier, a new layer of bark. Each time we moved away from our honesty and trust in one another, another layer of bark appeared. More separation. We don't see each other anymore. We see bark. We see hurts and weaknesses and mistrust. We see jealousies and labels. We choose to see the bark instead of each other, and when we rage at the bark we created, we create more."

"Can we get rid of it?" a voice asked.

"It has to burn off and it will hurt. It means being truly honest with ourselves and each other. Being vulnerable, trusting again. It means allowing, and forgiving each other for being human."

"How do you know this'll work?"

"I don't. I only know that I won't return to Yarrow without trying." The men lowered their faces at his son's name. "He'd be walking by now. I will not return to him as a man who didn't even try to climb back to what I once was... what I know I am. This way, I'll still return a better man than I am at this moment."

Heads nodded. "But how?"

"We make a choice. The bark is hard, and it will bring things to the surface we don't want to face. We have to choose each day to burn away the habits that don't serve us. Burn away the offense and suspicion, burn away the lies from the Hall. But none of us is alone; we'll do it together."

Hass moved toward the fire and dropped a piece of wood onto it. "So what's the plan?"

"We burn the bark together. We return to the Tunstream inside us before we return to Tunstream outside us. And we never forget that under the bark, we are still the coals."

epilogue

Yarrow's giggles wove through the new growth in the field, and flashes of his snow-white hair bobbed among the green stalks as he ran toward the stream at the end of the field.

A warm afternoon breeze brushed Kish's hair in front of her face and she tucked it behind her ears and called out to him, "You go ahead then and choose the spot."

Tabar leaned on the wooden fence beside her and chuckled. "When you're three summers old you can fit through these fences a lot easier than we can." Tabar grunted and forced himself through the rails, holding his arms out for Kish to use as support. Maya said not to expect her limp to get any better, but here she was climbing through a fence. She didn't know Kish like he did. He loved how when she smiled at him, the dimple on her cheek came to life, and seemed to dissolve the thick scar that ran from her cheekbone to the corner of her mouth. What the Hall had meant as a constant reminder of its strength only ever reminded him of Kish's.

As they stood, a squeal of delight reached them. Kish shielded her eyes from the sun's glare and looked over the field. "I believe your son has decided to play in the stream first and eat later." She pulled the strap of her satchel over her head and took Tabar's hand.

Tabar brushed his free hand against the tops of the crop as they moved toward the stream together. The healthy cycles of Tunstream's fields had returned, but the health of the villagers would take a little longer before they'd feel whole again. It was a hard and painful work. But they had kept their promise, and no one was doing it alone. That they were all stronger for what they'd endured seemed impossible, but it was true. Many things were that way now.

Yarrow's clothes lay discarded piece by piece in a trail that led toward the stream.

"Here looks good," Kish said. She sat and pulled bread and cheese from the satchel and watched Yarrow splash in the stream. "He'll come when he's hungry enough."

Tabar studied her face as she prepared their meal, hoping to remember every detail. She gave him a half smile. "I'm trying to pretend we have all the time in the world...but we don't."

"We have *this* moment. All we ever have is right now."

Kish nodded and checked on Yarrow again. Satisfied, she turned her attention to Tabar. "Isn't this campaign dangerous?"

"They all are."

"But this time you're infiltrating the guards at the Hall."

"That's the plan."

"I can't believe you've got guards all over the land throwing logs into fires and talking to each other."

Tabar shook his head with a smile. "Who would've thought? We just try to remind them of who they are. It's easy to forget when you're in pain."

Kish chewed the food in her mouth thoughtfully and watched the men gather on the road in the distance. They'd already said their goodbyes at the village square and were waiting for Tabar. "Is Hass going with you?"

"I rely on him now more than ever. He's a brave man."

Kish lifted his hand and kissed it. "But what if you are caught this time?"

"Then I guess I won't have to hide anymore. I'll be found."

You can find more of Lisa King's stories here - www.lisakingauthor.com/books

A NOTE FROM THE AUTHOR

Thanks for reading *Magic Man*. I hope you enjoyed Tabar's journey and that you'll continue to follow the character stories from Awenmell.

I truly appreciate the feedback I get from my readers. If you enjoy my stories, please consider leaving a review at your store of purchase and on review websites such as Goodreads. Reviews not only help other readers find books they might enjoy, they can be instrumental in a book's success. You can also share your Awenmell experience with friends on social media. 'Word of Mouth' books are always the best discoveries!

#awenmell #magicman

Tabar's story came to life in an unusual way. One of my early readers asked about a scene from my novel, *Crown of Fire*.

"I wonder how that guy got there. What led him to be right there, at that time?"

I hadn't considered writing a story about the 'Magic Man', yet the question about his history didn't leave me until Tabar's full story began to emerge.

In *Magic Man*, I hoped to show how our greatest potential is often hidden until called upon by circumstance, and also to highlight our interconnectedness. I wanted to focus on that moment in time shared between Tabar and 'The Idler', and how it altered both of their journeys, yet neither could have known how deeply they'd affected the other. I hope you enjoyed reading *Magic Man* and that you might look out for Tabar in the novel *Crown of Fire*.

Acknowledgements

Thanks again to my amazing support team. They let me call on them at all sorts of ridiculous hours, to sound out ideas and listen to my frustrations and doubts.

I'm forever grateful for the unending support of Michelle Capper, Amy Deamon, Trish O'Keeffe, Sarah Patterson, Lynda Pedder, Joanne Smith, and Ali Strachan. Heartfelt thanks to my husband Stewart, who patiently watches me pace out my ideas in the hallway, and always directs me into the forest when I need to recharge and reset.

I love you all.

This novella wouldn't exist without the talent of the following professionals.

Thanks a million, to Lauren Sapala for her insight and encouragement, Rebecca Hendry for her skillful editing, and Heather Musingo for her artwork and inspired cover design.

Thank you all so much.

ABOUT THE AUTHOR

Lisa King is a international award-winning author and amateur nature photographer who lives near Brisbane, Australia. When she's not writing, you can find her hiking though lush rainforests, and exploring the wide open spaces of the Scenic Rim, taking notes for her novels and capturing the diverse and complex ecosystems where she feels most at home.

Lisa loves to transport readers to worlds where the heroes have everyday struggles, flaws and inner conflicts, and the natural world is part of the nurturing and healing process. As an advocate for education and empathy for trauma survivors, Lisa hopes her books will encourage readers on their own healing paths.

You can connect with Lisa on social media @lisakingauthor and join her readers circle at www.lisakingauthor.com

Also by Lisa King

AWENMELL SERIES

Crown of Fire - Awenmell Series : Book One
Rise - Awenmell Series : Book Two

AWENMELL CHARACTER SERIES

Magic Man - Awenmell Characters 1
Eshnae - Awenmell Characters 2

STANDALONE NOVELS

Dandelion Wishes – The Untold Story of Coral
Maxwell-King